# MAORI TALES
## OF LONG AGO

By A. W. Reed
Illustrated by A. S. Paterson

Foreword by David Simmons

NEW
HOLLAND

This softcover edition published in 2014 by New Holland Publishers (NZ) Ltd
Auckland • Sydney • London

www.newhollandpublishers.com

5/39 Woodside Ave, Northcote, Auckland 0627, New Zealand
Unit 1, 66 Gibbes Street, Chatswood, NSW 2067, Australia
131-151 Great Titchfield Street, London WIW 5BB, United Kingdom

First published in 2010 by New Holland Publishers (NZ) Ltd

Copyright © 2014 in text: A. W. Reed Estate
Copyright © 2014 New Holland Publishers (NZ) Ltd
The A. W. Reed Estate has asserted its right to be identified as the author of this work.

Publishing manager: Christine Thomson
Commissioned by Louise Armstrong
Design: Justine Mackenzie

National Library of New Zealand Cataloguing-in-Publication Data

Reed, A. W. (Alexander Wyclif), 1908-1979.
Tales. Selections
Māori tales of long ago / by A.W. Reed ; illustrated by
A.S. Paterson ; foreword by David Simmons.
Collates all the stories originally published in Wonder tales of
Māoriland (1948) and Māori tales of long ago (1957), by A.W.
Reed with the original illustrations by A.S. Paterson.
ISBN 978-1-86966-423-7
1. Maori (New Zealand people)—Folklore.
2. Tales—New Zealand. [1. Maori (New Zealand people)—
Folklore. 2. Folklore—New Zealand.] [1. Pūrākau. reo 2.
Kōrero paki mā ngā tamariki. reo] I. Paterson, A. S. II. Title.
398.208999442—dc 23

10 9 8 7 6 5 4 3 2

Colour reproduction by Pica Digital, Pte Ltd., Singapore.
Printed in China by Toppan Leefung Printing Ltd., on paper sourced from sustainable forests.

All rights reserved. No part of this publication may be reproduced, stored in a retrieval system,
or transmitted in any form or by any means, electronic, mechanical, photocopying, recording or
otherwise, without the prior permission of the publishers and copyright holders.

While every care has been taken to ensure the information contained in this book is as accurate
as possible, the authors and publishers can accept no responsibility for any loss, injury or
inconvenience sustained by any person using the advice contained herein.

# CONTENTS

# FOREWORD

The tales in this book have been told over many hundreds of years. Some are stories that were told in the Pacific Islands long before the Māori ancestors came to Aotearoa. Many years ago, A. W. Reed gathered these myths and legends together as part of his wish to make Māori stories better known. Here he recounts them simply, as tales told by the wise village storyteller, genial old Pōpō, to the young son and daughter of the chief, Rata and Hine.

In the old days, it was children like Rata and Hine who attended the school of learning, the whare wānanga, to learn their tribe's genealogy, history, and the arts of war and peace. But during the winter, when fathers and warriors were away on expeditions, the old people stayed at home and taught the younger folk. As the old proverb has it:

Te tangata i akona ki te whare, tunga ki te marae tau ana
A person who has learnt in the house stands easily in the marae

A lot of the teaching was not, as it is today, sitting down and taking notes, but consisted of listening to stories. Recently, I was asked to talk to a group of people from Ōrākei marae in Auckland about the history of their tribal area. We looked at the places around us and were able to share the stories their names recalled. Motutapu Island in Auckland's Hauraki Gulf is named after Te Motutapu a Tinirau, 'Tinirau's sacred island', and Tinirau had a pet whale, Tutunui. Kae's stealing and eating of that whale is one of the stories in this book.

In 1845, the governor of New Zealand, George Grey, found that in order to understand what the chiefs were saying, he needed to not only speak Māori but also to understand the references the speakers were making to ancient poems, proverbs and stories. On marae, references are made to these tales. A speaker will greet the roof above as Ranginui, the Sky Father, and the floor below as Papatūānuku, the Earth Mother, and the house in between as Tānewhakapiripiri, Tāne clinging closely, referring to the time before Papa and Rangi were separated when their children, including the god of forests, Tāne, clung close to them. The story of Papa and Rangi's separation is told in this book, in the tale 'How light came into the world'. As with any farewell, their parting caused Rangi and his beloved great sadness and this is why rain falling from the sky to the earth is called roimata, or in full, ngā roimata a Rangi, the tears of the Sky Father, while mist rising from the earth is known as ngā roimata a Papa mo Ranginui, the tears of the Earth Mother for her husband far above her.

Māui the trickster is known from Hawai'i to Aotearoa. After Rangi the Sky Father and Papa the Earth Mother were separated it was Māui who sailed on the seas and hauled up the islands Tonga (South) and Rarotonga (Under-South) then finally another island, his fish, Te Ika a Māui, the North Island of Aotearoa.

Māui is the one who found or made many things in this world. These things are a gift from him to us. All we have to do is listen to the stories and give a gift in return, the gift or koha of using our brains. The story of Māui catching the sun is told here in Aotearoa. Why? The ancestors came from the tropics and that story tells of the change in time and the change in the main stars used to navigate canoes to our southern seas.

Why are these tales told again and again? They are good stories, which also tell us how the ancestors and their world came to be. They tell us how the ancestors came to Aotearoa and how to respect the guardians of our world. Lastly, the tales remind us to enjoy living in the world they have made.

David Simmons, 2009
*Former ethnologist and Assistant Director, Auckland War Memorial Museum*

# HOW MAUI WENT FISHING

RATA sat on a branch of the pohutukawa tree, rubbing his back against the trunk, not thinking about anything. The sunlight danced on the waves far below like points of fire, while the leaves and the crimson flowers swayed gently in the breeze. Some of the branches creaked as they rubbed against each other, almost drowning the soft hiss of the little waves on the beach.

Presently the boy sat up and looked round, and he heard other sounds. The women were laughing and talking as they worked in the kumara patch. Some of the men had gone into the forest to snare birds, and others were out fishing. He raised himself a little higher and saw the big canoes looking like twigs lying out on the water far beyond the headland. Nearer to him a ridge of land stretched out like a long neck and swelled into a head fringed with the big timbers of the palisades that surrounded his father's village.

On the narrow strip of beach below the pa or village, Rata heard voices. He pushed aside a branch and leaned over. Yes, there were two people there. One was a young girl. It was his sister, Hine. The other was a man, tall and fat, so fat that he seemed to roll from side to side as he walked.

In a flash Rata swung off the branch and began to climb down the cliff. A shout of alarm came from the fat man. "Silly old Popo," Rata said to himself with a smile, and waved his hand. In a little while he slid on to the beach, bringing a tiny landslide of stones with him. Popo wagged his head, pretending to be angry. "It is not brave to come down the cliff like that," he said. "You think you are a warrior, like your father, but you are only a silly boy bringing sorrow to your family. You will kill yourself some day."

Rata caught his sister's eye and smiled. Hine had often scrambled down the steep slope with him, swinging from the roots of the trees that had burrowed through the ground and then thrust themselves out into the sunshine.

"Yes, he is a foolish boy," Hine said, taking the old man's hand in hers. "But he will not come to harm. Let us forget what may never happen and come for a swim."

The three of them ran down to the water and waded out until the cool waves swirled around their waists. They threw themselves forward and the sea lifted them as they swam farther out to where a black reef of rock lay in the middle of the bay. Popo was like a fish in the water. He swam with long strokes, never hurrying. He was so fat that he rode high in the water. While Rata and Hine were still swimming he reached the reef and began to pull himself up on the rocks. Brother and sister stopped to laugh at him.

"He is just like a fish out of water," Rata said.

Popo had grasped a piece of seaweed, but his hand slipped and with a terrific splash he toppled backwards into the water. He came up quickly, laughing at himself, and soon managed to find an easier way out of the water. When Rata and Hine reached the reef, he stretched out his hands and helped to pull them up the slippery rocks.

For a long while they all lay quiet in the sunshine, so that the water ran off them in little streams, and then their bodies dried and grew warm. Rata turned over on his face with his toes dabbling in a rock pool where tiny sea creatures darted to and fro. His head hung over the edges of the rocks so he could see down into the clear water. Long trailers of seaweed brushed backwards and forwards as the waves surged in and rushed out to sea again. The water heaped itself up like a moving mountain, swelling close to Rata's face. For a moment

*With a terrific splash Popo toppled back into the water*

the seaweed seemed to lie still, and Rata could see down a long tunnel which grew darker until there was nothing to see but blackness.

"It's like looking into a dark cave here," he said sleepily. "You can pretend that there might be anything at the bottom of it."

"Perhaps there is," said Popo, who was lying flat on his back, looking over his stomach at the pohutukawas on the cliff. "There might be another world down there."

"How could there be another world?" Hine said. "Only fish live there."

"There could be lots of things down there," Popo said again. "If you look very hard you might even be able to see a house."

The children laughed at him. "No one would ever find a house at the bottom of the sea!" Rata said scornfully.

Popo sat up. "You children have many things to learn," he said seriously. "Why, it was Maui who found a house at the bottom of the sea. And if he hadn't found that house, and a big fish, we should not be sitting on this rock today."

"Is it a story?" asked Hine.

"Yes," Popo replied, "it is a story that you should know."

With a little sigh of happiness the children found a more comfortable position. Popo was the loveliest story-teller in the village.

"Be quiet," Popo said. "This is the story of Maui and the great fish that he caught."

\* \* \*

Maui woke up very early one morning, long before the sun had risen. He crept quietly from his sleeping-mat and patted his favourite fish-hook. It was inlaid with mother-of-pearl, and deep magic lay under its polished surface.

Shutting the door of the house behind him, he walked across the wet sand and climbed into his brother's canoe. He lifted the bottom boards and slipped into the narrow space beneath, pulling the boards over him so that he could not be seen.

*The magic fish-hook*

8

Presently he heard voices as his brothers came nearer. They piled their fishing lines into the canoe and launched it into the smooth water. Then came the sound of the paddles, and jeering laughter. "We have got rid of Maui, the tiny one, anyway," one of them said. "He is a nuisance. He will be very angry when he wakes up and finds we have gone without him."

"Maui is not sleeping," said Maui in a deep voice. His brothers looked round in astonishment. Surely that had sounded just like Maui! They peered over the side, but he was not there.

"Perhaps it is a gull," one of them said, but they did not believe him. Maui, lying under their feet, laughed to himself.

For a little while there was no sound except the cool splashing noise of the paddles. Then the brothers stopped. Somewhere they heard a chuckling noise. There were no birds to be seen. The sound came from under the canoe. They looked right under it but nothing could be hid in the clear water. One of them pulled up the floorboards, and there sat Maui, grinning like a goblin.

"Maui!" they all cried in dismay. "We will not take you with us. You will do something silly and spoil our fishing."

"Oh yes, you will take me," Maui said.

"No, there is plenty of time. We will go back and put you ashore."

Maui frowned. "It is too late, brothers," he said. "Look behind you."

They turned round and looked in astonishment, because there was no land to be seen. All they could see was the great ocean and the sun shining on the empty waters. Maui grinned again.

*There was no land to be seen*

"Now you can see that nothing will stop me," he said. "I have brought my magic fish-hook, the one made from the jawbone of my grandmother." He lifted it up and turned it till it flashed in the sunshine. "Magic runs through it when I hold it," he said. "It has stretched out the ocean. Look, it leaps in my hand. Today will be lucky for fishing, brothers. Take up your paddles."

The sun was high when Maui, who had been sitting on the floorboards holding the magic fish-hook to his ear as if he could hear it speak, called to his brothers to stop paddling.

"Here is the place where we shall get a good catch. Throw out your lines."

The brothers were too frightened to say anything. They baited their hooks and lowered them into the water, and in a little while a pile of shining fish lay in the canoe.

"This is very good, Maui," said the eldest. "You have brought us to a good place. Now we shall go home."

"Oh no," Maui replied. "Now it is my turn. Give me some bait."

"No, we will not give you any bait," they all cried together, because they were afraid of what he would do next.

Maui said nothing. He struck his nose, and when the blood flowed, he smeared it over the white bone hook, and lowered it into the water. Down, down, down, went the hook at the end of the flax line. At first they could see it gleaming in the water like a moon-beam, and then it slipped out of sight. At last the line went slack and Maui pulled it gently. The line grew taut. "Ha! I have caught a fish," he shouted. "Now you will see the fishing of Maui, the little one."

Far down under the water, in the world where the sea-god lives, the sacred fish-hook had caught in the doorway of the house of Tonganui, the son of the sea-god. Ah, my children, that was where Tonganui lived, he and all his people, never dreaming that Maui's white hook would come stealing through the shadowy water from the world of air and fire above the sea.

Maui took the strain on his line. He braced his feet on the sides of the canoe and pulled with all his might until Tonganui's house groaned with the strain. There was a sudden jerk as Maui pulled the house up from the seabed, and with it came a great piece of land.

Maui sang a magic song that makes heavy weights light. His brothers drove the paddles deep into the water. The flax cord and the white hook sang as they lifted up the house of Tonga. It came close to the surface and then the carved wooden figure on top jumped out of the water like a fish. Maui kept on pulling. The house rose above the water. There was the magic hook, held tight in the doorway. Then came the land underneath, shining like a great fish with its tail stretching far away to where the sky meets the sea.

It was Maui's fish.

"Stay here," Maui said to his brothers. "Don't make a sound. The sea-god is angry because I have stolen the house of his son. I must make peace with him. When I come back we will share this fish of mine."

He ran along the back of the fish. Maui's brothers could hardly believe what they had seen. "It is real," one of them said. "See, it is a great land that our little brother has found."

Ah, smooth and bright and shining was the land that Maui pulled from beneath the sea. On it were houses, and smoking fires. Birds were singing and streams were chattering down its sides. "This piece belongs to me," one of the brothers shouted.

"No, it is mine," cried another.

"I shall take this bit," said a third. They all jumped out of the canoe and ran about the land, slashing it with their weapons. The great Fish felt their running feet and woke from sleep. It

*Tonganui, son of the sea-god*

tossed on the water, and its smooth surface was ruffled and broken into hills and valleys. Maui was angry when he came back, but it was too late. If they had left it alone it would be smooth to this very day.

It happened long, long ago, this fishing of Maui. If you could climb up to the first heaven and look down on our land, you would see that it is the shape of a fish. Far away in the south is its head, far away in the north is its tail. In the middle is Taupo Moana, its heart. This is our country, our great Fish of Maui.

# THE BIRTH OF MAUI

RATA and Hine had climbed down to the rocks where the big waves crashed against the headland. Father had said that he was going out with the fishermen in the big canoe towards the island of Taranga. The canoe had left early in the morning and the children had hurried down to see it go past. They had a favourite spot above the waves, where the spray sometimes dashed in their faces. When they got to the place they found that their old friend Popo was already sitting there. He was too old to go out with the fishermen or to go on the war trail, but he loved to see the canoe speeding out of the harbour with flashing paddles and to hear the chant of the paddlers.

The children were glad to see Popo because he was always ready to tell them a story. But the story had to wait until the canoe had gone past. A big wave rushed between the rocks and curled over with a tremendous crash, sending up a great mass of foam and water and a cloud of spray which tasted salty on their lips.

"This is more like the Taitamatane," said Popo.

"Taitamatane! The Sea of Men!" said Rata. "What does that mean, Popo?"

"That is the name for the west coast," Popo said. "There are not many harbours here, Rata, and with the westerly winds behind them the long waves crash and thunder against the cliffs and beaches of that coast. Some day you will see for yourself. It is the kind of sea which needs strong men at the paddles of the canoe.

"This coast of ours is sunny and sheltered. There are many harbours like ours, with sandy beaches and trees growing almost in the water. So we call it

12

the Sea of Women. It is a wonderful place for fishing – but today the sea-god is angry. It is the kind of day when strong men must be at the paddles of the canoe."

"Here it is!" shouted Hine. They stood up to watch. It was a wonderful sight. The harbour was like a great round calabash or bowl, with a tiny entrance guarded by rocks, so that you could throw a stone from one side to another. Inside the harbour was calm and sheltered, but the sea roared and fought with the rocks at the entrance.

They heard the sound of the paddlers' chant as the canoe came closer. A little white wave rose above the bow in the smooth water, and then the carved bowpiece began to rise and fall. Soon the canoe reached the narrow opening. The chant of the paddlers grew louder, the waves crashed against the sides of the canoe and the steersman strained to hold it straight and true. At one moment the great vessel pointed at the sky, slid over the crest of the wave and sank into the trough of the waters. The children could see it below them.

They looked down at the men and saw the deck of manuka sticks, the narrow seats, the neatly coiled fishing lines, and the shining hooks.

They made no sound, but looked proudly at their father as he stood in the prow, watching for the rock that lay beneath the surface of the water. Another giant wave lifted the canoe again. It swung on the crest, and as it slid down the far side father gave a signal. The men on one side dipped their paddles deeply in the smooth water and the steersman braced himself to take the strain. The canoe leaned sideways, turned towards them for a second and then raced out into the open sea.

Popo sat down in his own special place where the waves had long ago worn a smooth channel which was wide enough for his fat body.

"A sea for men!" he said again. "More than one canoe has been smashed to pieces here."

For a while they were all silent, watching the canoe grow smaller and smaller until it was like an insect with moving legs walking over the water. There were times when it was hidden by the big rollers, but always it climbed the hills of water until at last it was only a speck in the distance.

The children scrambled amongst the rocks, watching the kelp surge in on the waves and then double over itself and draw quickly back towards the sea, over and over again. Amongst the broken shells and pebbles on a tiny beach nearby, they found the shells of sea-urchins and pieces of driftwood carved into strange shapes by the waves. Hine found a smooth brown thing which she took to Popo.

The old man had been asleep and he opened his eyes drowsily. "It's a nut," he said. "It doesn't come from our own land. The wind and the waves have washed it for thousands of miles across the ocean and at last it has reached our own village. That was how Maui was once washed ashore. Do you remember what I told you about him yesterday?"

"Of course we remember. Tell us more about him, Popo. Was he a god?"

"Well, a kind of god," Popo said. "He was partly man and partly god. He was a merry fellow. He did a lot of good, but to some people he did some harm. Would you like to hear another story about him?"

"Yes, please," said the brother and sister together. "Did he really come ashore like this nut?"

"Yes, just like this nut. Perhaps this is the best way to tell a story like this, while the sea throws all sorts of things on to the shore at our feet."

\* \* \*

Let us travel in our minds far over the sea, out of sight of the land. There was only blue sky above, and blue waves underneath. The sky rested on the very edges of the sea and in the middle a bundle of seaweed rose and fell on the long swell of the ocean. Above it, the seabirds circled round and round, crying and flapping their wings. Now and again one of them flew down and pecked at the bundle and flew away.

In the middle of the seaweed there was a tangle of hair and in the middle of this, like a young bird in a nest, lay a tiny baby. He kicked his legs and gave happy little cries as he lay in his gently rocking cradle. Underneath him were the deep waters where the huge sea monsters swam and fought and preyed on smaller fish, but the baby knew nothing about them. The sun warmed him and the seagulls sang a strange lullaby as they soared and fluttered over the floating cradle.

The baby was Maui. He was just a tiny little scrap of a thing. Because his mother did not know he was alive, she had cut off her hair and wrapped him in it and pushed him gently to another land. The waves washed him on to a soft bed of sand.

The baby kicked away the seaweed and the clinging strands of hair, and lay there happily. But soon clouds covered the sun, and the land birds looked at him hungrily. Flies buzzed round and the wind was cold. Baby Maui began to cry. He could not understand what was happening to him, and gave a piercing wail.

Not far away from where the baby lay lived Tama, who was a god of the sea. He had built his house on the cliffs where he could look out across the great ocean. He had not seen the little bundle of seaweed and jellyfish washed ashore, but he had heard the cry of the baby. He looked everywhere but he could see nothing except the heap of seaweed on the sand.

"That is strange," said Tama to himself. "Why should the gulls keep flying over it? I had better go and have a look at it."

He went down the steep path and along the beach until he came to the heap of seaweed. He bent over it, and again he heard the cry of a baby, but although it was close, it was very faint now. Tama picked off the jellyfish and pulled the fronds of seaweed away. There was little Maui, nearly dead with the cold.

He took the baby up in his arms and hurried back to his home. It was cold inside the whare. Tama tied little Maui to the rafters and put more wood on the fire. The warm air rose upwards and the baby began to cough and move his arms and legs. Presently he felt more comfortable and began to laugh. Tama took him down, wrapped him in a soft feather cloak, and put him to sleep in the corner.

This was Maui's first adventure, though he was too young to remember it. Tama was very glad to have someone with him in his lonely house, even though it was only a baby. He soon found that he did not have so much time to spend looking at the sea. Babies need a great deal of care and have to be looked after. They cannot do anything for themselves. Tama was kept busy looking after Maui, pounding food so that it was soft and easy to eat, talking to him and playing games with him.

Maui grew quickly. As soon as he was able to toddle he went outside and held out his arms to the birds which fluttered down and played with him. Tama used to stand at the door and smile at the little boy. Somehow the birds seemed to understand what Maui said to them. They let him pull their

*The magic that old Tama taught him*

*Maui goes fishing*  page 11

feathers and roll them over and over in the grass. Tama loved his little boy, and as he grew tall and strong they spent long hours together. Tama taught him the wisdom of the sea – how fishes lived and spoke to each other. He told him how other people lived; how they worked, and hunted for birds and fish, how they grew kumaras in their gardens and dug fern root and gathered berries. He told stories of battles and raids, and of how men and women danced and sang in the great meeting houses at night. Maui loved to hear these things. Best of all was the magic that old Tama taught him when the firelight flickered on the walls and the carved figures of his house at night, and the stars twinkled outside. He listened to everything that Tama told him and stored it up in his mind.

The friendship he had for the birds of the sea and the forest as a little boy grew stronger as the years passed by. He knew their names and their habits. When some of them flew across the thousands of miles of ocean in the spring, they came to greet their friend Maui.

"All my life I shall love you," Maui said. "We will always be friends," and the birds flew round him and twittered, "Friends."

"You have been a good boy to one who is your father yet not your father," Tama said one night. "You think you will stay here forever because I have been like a father and a mother to you, but you are growing up, and soon you will go away. I can feel it in these old bones."

"What will you do when I go away?" Maui asked him.

"I will sit in the veranda of my house and look over the sea as I did before you came, Maui. I will remember how the waves brought you to me when you were a baby. I will remember the games we played together, and how you made friends with birds and fishes. I will remember the deep magic I taught you, and I will watch you still, not with these old eyes of mine which do not see very well now, but with the eyes of the spirit. What will you do, Maui?"

"I will go to my own people. I will be a man."

"Yes," Tama said. "You will go to your own people. You will leave the old man who has taught you so much. You will do many wonderful things, Maui. Some people will love you and some will be impatient, because you are some-times mischievous and cruel. Try not to hurt others. Do good and I will say the magic spells that will keep you from harm."

17

"Yes, I will try to do good," Maui said, really meaning it. But we shall see that he could never be good for very long, and Tama knew this too.

"You will play many tricks, but I know you will do good things as well. Remember then old Tama who loved you."

Another summer came and Maui had grown into a young man, but Tama was old and bent. "You must go now, Maui," he said. "Soon I will go to the leaping place, into the underworld, where I will find the friends of my boyhood. It is not right for you to stay here any longer."

Maui was sorry to have to say good-bye to his old friends, but he was anxious to go out into the world where there were others who were young like himself. Tama raised his hands over him in blessing and Maui ran down the path that led into the forest. He skipped and jumped with excitement. For once he had no time to talk to the birds.

"Stop and play with us, Maui," they sang, but he took no notice. The leaves of the trees brushed against him and the supplejack tried to trip him up, but he pushed them aside.

*"You must go now, Maui"*

All day long he ran, down into the valleys and up the hilltops, stopping only to drink from the little streams. He crossed a wide plain, and climbed a hill. From the top he could see the country spread out below him, with lakes and rivers and forests, and far away he saw houses, and smoke going up in the still air. He knew that these were his people and that the little village was his home. Perhaps his mother had lit the fire for the evening meal.

He plunged down the hillside, running faster than ever. Darkness fell, but somewhere he could hear

**18**

voices singing, and they guided him onwards. There was a clear space in front of the house and in one of them he could see a light. He peeped round the open door and saw that there was a fire burning on the floor. There were four young men there, all taller and older than himself, and further away a beautiful woman whom he was sure must be his mother.

He slipped inside the house like a shadow and sat down behind the young men without being seen.

Presently his mother came over to the young men and said, "Stand up when I call you, so that we may dance. Maui-taha!"

The tallest of the young men stood up and said, "I am ready, Mother."

"That's one," she said.

"Maui-rota. That's two.

"Maui-pae. That's three.

"Maui-waho. That's four.

"All my sons are ready."

Then our Maui stood up and came out of the shadows. "I am Maui, too," he said.

His mother looked at him in surprise. "Oh no, you are not Maui. All my sons are here. I counted them myself."

"Yes, I am Maui," the boy said again. "These are my brothers. See, I know their names: Maui-taha, Maui-rota, Maui-pae, and Maui-waho. Now I have come, and I am Maui the littlest one."

"I have never seen you before," his mother replied, while Maui-taha, Maui-rota, Maui-pae and Maui-waho stared at him. "No, you cannot be Maui, little stranger. I have no other sons."

"Are you sure, my mother?"

She thought. "Yes, there was one, a tiny little baby, so small that the wind would have blown him away. But we shall never see him again, for he is dead. Where do you come from, stranger?"

His mother picked up a burning log from the fire and held it close to his face.

"What is my name?" she asked.

"You are my mother. Your name is Taranga."

Her eyes filled with tears. She leaned forward and clasped him in her arms. "Yes, you are indeed my little Maui," she said. "I have found you again. You

are the youngest Maui and I shall call you
Maui-tikitiki-a-Taranga.* You will live here
with your brothers and you will be my
own little son again."

And so it was that Maui came
to his mother's home and lived
with his brothers. But he was
not always popular, for he was
a born mischief. He was clever,
too, and clever people are not
always popular. When kites were
being flown, Maui's kite always
flew highest. When they played
tag, which they called *wi*, Maui
always ran the fastest. When darts
were being thrown, Maui's fern
frond always went the farthest. At
the breath-holding game Maui could

*"You are my mother"*

always recite the longest. At swimming and diving he was always best. He
was a friend of all the forest folk, and because of the magic he had learned
from Tama, he could turn himself into a bird and escape from his brothers
when they were angry with him.

Because he was clever and better at games than his brothers, they were
often annoyed with him. But Maui did not mind. He laughed merrily and
went off to play with his friends the birds, and practised the magic that Tama
had taught him.

\* \* \*

"What happened to him when he grew up?" Rata asked.

"Oh ho, that is another story," Popo chuckled. "Think of how he came,
children, not what happened afterwards. Every time you see something
strange brought up by the sea, remember little Maui who came ashore on a
big wave wrapped in his mother's hair – remember Maui-tikitiki-a-Taranga."

*Maui-in-the-topknot-of-Taranga.

# MAUI IN THE UNDERWORLD

RATA had been in a mischievous mood all day. Before it was light in the big sleeping-house, he had pulled off his sister's mat. Then he had run away when mother wanted him to gather dry sticks for the fire, and had made her angry.

"If father were here you wouldn't dare to go off like that," Hine had said. But father was away from home, leading a war-party on a raid.

Rata had been such a nuisance that everyone was glad when he left the pa and went away somewhere by himself. Everyone except Popo, and Popo didn't know what was going to happen to him.

After the morning meal he had gone down the steep road from the pa and walked around the beach to the other side of the harbour. Although he was big and fat, Popo could walk very quietly. He was thinking of food, and Rata knew that he had gone into the forest to see whether there were berries on the trees. If there were plenty of berries the birds would grow fat. Kereru, the wood pigeon, would bring all his brothers and sisters into the forests and when the warriors came back, the hunters would take their long spears and set their traps by the streams, and would kill thousands of the birds. They would be roasted and packed in baskets made of bark and covered with boiling fat and kept for the hungry days of the winter.

Popo was pleased with what he had seen. The trees were heavily laden with berries and already the wood pigeons were growing fat. He had been along most of the forest paths, treading so lightly and carefully that the feeding birds were not disturbed. As the sun sank low in the west he hurried back towards the pa. The trees thinned out and he could see the water glowing like fire in the red sunset rays. Up above, a flock of kakas screamed and chattered as they flew towards the hills. Popo looked up at them as he hurried down towards the beach.

The next moment he was lying flat on his face gasping for breath. Presently he sat up, feeling himself carefully to see if any bones were broken.

"Strange," he said, for Popo was fond of talking, and had little conversations with himself when there was no one else to listen to him. "I'm sure I heard someone laughing."

He listened carefully, but there was no sound except the distant screaming of the kakas and the rustling wind in the branches of the trees. Popo sat as still as a carved image. Down by the water's edge there was a plop as a fish leaped out of the water and fell back again.

Then came the sound he had been listening for – a faint echoing laughter far away through the trees. The hairs on Popo's neck rose and he felt frightened. "Fairies!" he said aloud and shivered. Everyone knew that the strange fairy people, who ate no cooked food and came out only at night, lived somewhere in the hills on the south side of the harbour. They had even been seen near the beach below the forest – and the shadows were creeping through the trees.

Popo stood up and peered fearfully into the forest. His foot hurt and he glanced down. He bent down quickly and drew a sharp breath. A strong flax leaf was stretched from one tree to another. This was not the work of fairies but of someone darker-skinned. A suspicion came into his mind and, forgetting his twisted foot, he limped quickly down to the beach. He was just in time to see a small boy climbing over the rocks at the end of the beach, before he dropped out of sight on the far side.

Popo was angry. He hobbled along the sand, climbed over the rocks, crossed the creek, and went along the path that wound through the trees and up the hill to the pa. It was a long walk and as he went Popo felt his anger leaving him. The water had eased his ankle and, as he came in sight of the pa, he gave a little chuckle.

"I was a naughty little boy myself once," he said. "I wonder who the rascal was!"

Presently Rata came out of the gateway and stood looking down towards him.

"Is that you, Popo?"

"It is me," Popo replied, puffing a little as he climbed the steep path. "What do you want, Rata?"

"I was looking for you. I wondered where you were."

"You knew I was over in the forest, little one. Did you miss me?"

"I was worried when it began to get dark."

He put his hand in the old man's and walked by his side.

"Were you thinking of a flax leaf stretched between two trees, Rata?"

The boy hung his head. "I'm sorry, Popo. I did it for a trick, and I laughed when you fell. I didn't think you would see me. But when you were so long coming home I thought you must have been hurt."

A tear trickled down his nose and he wiped it away with the back of his hand.

"It was a foolish thing to do," Popo said. "Anyone might have been hurt, but you knew that it was old Popo who would fall. I might have broken my neck."

Rata sniffed, but the tears rolled more quickly down his face. Popo could see that the little boy was ashamed of what he had done.

"Are you really sorry, Rata?"

"I am sorry, Popo," he said, and began to cry. The old man bent over him and smiled.

"If you were not sorry I should be angry. For a while my heart was sad and I would have beaten you, but now I can see that you loved Popo all the time and it was only the foolishness of a little boy. Dry your tears, Rata, for a young warrior does not cry. All is well between you and me."

*The flax baskets of steaming kumara and fish were handed round by the women*

They came to the big open place in front of the houses as the flax baskets of steaming kumara and fish were handed round by the women. Rata said nothing during the meal, but

**23**

afterwards Popo and Rata and his sister found a quiet corner of the meeting house.

The old man stretched himself out on the floor, half leaning against the wall.

"Boys and girls can be naughty sometimes," he said, "but I think that they are really very fond of older people. Maui was like that, but he never grew up properly, so people did not understand him. Do you remember the time he dropped berries on his father and mother in the forest?"

"Please tell us," Rata said.

"Yes, this is just the right sort of night for a Maui story," Hine said.

* * *

After he had been living with his brothers for some time, Maui found that they were not merry or kindly people. They were older than he was and wouldn't play with him. When he played tricks on them, thinking they would laugh, they became angry and hit him, and said, "No one asked you to come here. We don't want you. Go away, Maui, you little nuisance."

Then Maui would laugh and poke fun at them. He went off into the forest and played with his friends the birds, who loved him.

There was only one thing that made Maui feel really unhappy. There were other boys living in the pa, and they all had fathers, but Maui had never seen his father. No one would tell him about his father and sometimes he wondered whether he had one.

And then there was something he couldn't understand about his mother. He never saw her in the daytime, and because he was so lonely he had to find his friends in the forest, amongst the feathered creatures. At night, when everyone went into the whare, his mother was there. He slept beside her on a little mat which his mother put beside her. When he woke up in the morning his mother had gone and he did not see her all day. Her sleeping mat was rolled up, and Maui had no one to talk to, for his brothers were always far too busy to take notice of him.

"Where does Mother go in the daytime?" he asked his brothers.

"How should we know?" they said.

"Because you have known her so much longer than I have," Maui said.

The brothers turned away. "She may go north, or south, or east, or west. We do not know and we do not care. Find out for yourself."

24

*He took the baby up in his arms*    page 15

*He played with his friends, the birds*

"Yes, that's what I will do," Maui said to himself. "They don't want to know because they don't love her, but I must find out what happens to her. If I know where she goes in the daytime, perhaps I will be able to find my father."

The next night Maui lay awake when the fire died down in the sleeping-house. He heard his mother breathing quietly and knew that she was asleep. Then he got up and crept to her side. He picked up her beautiful girdle and cloak and hid them under his sleeping-mat. Going softly on tiptoe, he went to the window and the door and blocked up the cracks where the light would creep in when morning came.

At daybreak, when she heard the song of the birds outside, Maui's mother woke up and looked around her to see whether it was light. Outside the clouds were tinged with pink, but inside the whare it was as dark as night. She lay back and went to sleep again. A long time after she woke up a second time, and listened. The birds were not singing as loudly as before, but a long ray of sunshine came through a hole in the roof and made a pool of light on the floor. Maui's mother jumped up and opened the window. The golden sunlight was everywhere. She looked for her girdle and apron, but could not see them because they were under Maui's mat. Without waiting to search for them, his mother threw an old cloak around her shoulders and ran outside.

Maui had tried to keep awake, but his eyes had closed long before, and he was fast asleep. It was the light coming in through the open door and window that wakened him. He opened his eyes just in time to see his mother closing the door behind her. He ran outside and saw his mother outside the village fence, in the long grass beside the path. Hiding behind the great post of the gateway, he saw her stoop and pull up a tussock of grass. A lump of earth came up with it, and underneath there must have been a big hole or pit, because the woman jumped in to it and pulled the clod on top of her.

Maui ran back to the whare, where his brothers were now awake, gathered round the window and wondering who had stuffed grass into the cracks.

"I have seen where mother goes in the daytime," he shouted excitedly. "She has gone into a hole in the ground!"

"You silly boy, that is one of the ways into the underworld, where men and women live far under the ground," his elder brother replied. "What does it matter where she goes so long as she leaves us plenty to eat?"

"But I want to be with her," Maui said. "If she is in the underworld, perhaps

26

she could show us where our father is. Perhaps she is with him now! Let us follow her at once."

The brothers looked at Maui scornfully. "What do we care where she is?" one of them said. "Rangi, the Great Heaven, is our father and Papa, the Earth, is our mother. If our true mother loved us she would not leave us."

"But I love her," Maui said. "She is my mother. She brings us food and stays with us at night and loves us. I will find her."

He went to his sleeping-mat and drew out his mother's clothes which he had hidden during the night. He tied the apron round his waist and put the feathered cloak around his shoulders. Then he said some magic words he had once heard, and he began to grow smaller. He slipped his arms inside the girdle, which covered him right up to the chin. He began to change in shape. His nose grew longer until it looked like a beak, his eyes became small and round, and his mouth disappeared. The only other part of him that showed was his feet. While the brothers watched in amazement, they turned into claws. The apron glowed with green and purple in the sunlight, and the beautiful white feathers of the cloak shone like the plumage of a wood pigeon.

"Look!" cried the eldest brother. "Maui has turned into a kereru!"

It was true. By magic spells Maui had changed himself into a forest bird. He spread his arms which had turned into strong beating wings and soared over his brothers' heads, over the tall fence, and glided into the long grass. He lifted the tuft of grass in his beak and plunged into the hole underneath.

It was dark when the earth settled over his head but soon his eyes became used to the gloom and he saw that he was in a narrow cave which sloped steeply

*"Maui has turned into a kereru"*

27

downwards. Maui flew down it, through the winding passages that led to the underworld. After he had flown for a long time he came to a strange and beautiful country. Trees grew there, tall and leafy, but no wind stirred their branches. Far above was a sky of polished rock, and the only thing that moved was a stream which flowed beneath the trees.

Maui flew up and perched himself on a branch of a tall karaka tree, and looked round him.

For a time everything was still, and then he saw some men and women in the distance. As they came closer, Maui saw that his mother was among them, and by her side was a tall man, who must surely be his father. They walked closer until they were right underneath him, and sat down on the ground. Maui bent his neck and picked a berry from a twig, and dropped it, so that it fell on his father's head.

His mother said, "The berry must have been dropped by a bird."

"No," said his father. "It was ripe and its time for falling had come."

Maui picked a cluster of the berries and jerked them with his beak so that they scattered as they fell, and hit both his mother and father. This time they knew that the berries must have been thrown at them. They sprang to their feet, while others hurried up to see what was happening.

"Look," someone shouted. "This is not a bird of the underworld. It has come from the place where the sun shines."

Everyone could see Maui now, and they wondered, because his white feathers and shining breast were so much brighter than the plumage of the birds of that land.

Some of the men threw stones at the pigeon and tried to knock it off the perch, but Maui dodged from side to side so that none of the stones hit him.

After a while, Maui's father picked up a stone and threw it. Maui saw it coming and at once tumbled off his perch and fluttered down to the ground. As he fell he grew bigger and less like a bird. He grew once again into a tall and handsome young man, with his mother's beautiful cloak hanging from his shoulders and the apron round his waist.

Taranga, his mother, knew him at once.

"This is my son," she said to her husband. "It is not Maui-taha, my first-born. It is not Maui-rota, my second. It is not Maui-pae, the third. It is not Maui-waho, the fourth. It is my little Maui, our youngest son, Maui-tikitiki-a-

28

Taranga." She threw her arms round him. "It is he who loves us best of all our children, for he has come bravely into the underworld to find us. Maui, this is your father, Makea-tu-tara, who loves you too."

Makea put his hand on his son's shoulder. "I can see you are brave, and the son of a chief. Some day you will be a great chief yourself, and I shall be proud of you. Greetings, my son."

Maui walked beside his father and mother to their home. He was very glad that he had found his father, and had seen for himself how tall and straight and handsome he was.

"Maui is the child who came by wind and wave," Taranga said to Makea.

"He will bring joy and sorrow into the world. He will tie up the sun, and bring many good things to his people. Some day he will fight the terrible goddess of death, and perhaps he will conquer her."

Maui was happy, for now his mother and father lived with their own people, and everyone knew that he was their son. Even the birds of the forest were glad. To show that they loved him, the wood pigeons wore the glowing colours of his mother's apron on their snow-white breasts.

\* \* \*

"That, my children, is how Maui found his father. Perhaps it would have been a good thing if he had always been kind and loving. But then he would not have been the Maui we know so well. There was not much love lost between him and his brothers; and other people became impatient with him because he was never still but was always thinking up a practical joke of some kind. But remember that he loved his mother!"

Popo sighed. "Perhaps we can't help being what we are," he said. "If he had always been good and kind we mightn't be telling stories about him in the whare at night. But we can always try to be good and never hurt other people with our silly jokes."

"No," Rata said. "Never again."

# HOW LIGHT CAME INTO THE WORLD

HINE poked her sharp elbow into Rata's side.
"Are you awake?" she whispered.

Rata turned over and opened his eyes. It was dark in the sleeping-house, but there was a faint red glow under the grey ashes of the fire.

"What's the matter?" he asked.

"Wake up," Hine said in a whisper, putting her finger to her lips. "Don't you remember? We are going to see the fish spearing."

Rata turned down his sleeping-mat.

"Come on then," he said, putting on his short waist mat. The children tip-toed through the whare. Rata pushed the sliding door open a little way. They crept through it and closed it behind them.

It was cold outside and there was no moon, but the stars were shining brightly. Like two shadows they flitted between the whares and came to the first palisade. There was one place where two of the posts were wider apart than the others. The gap was too small for men, but the children wriggled through.

They looked up at the tall watch-tower, where the sentry stood looking out towards the sea.

Hine gave a squeal of delight. "It's Popo," she whispered. Rata called to him softly: "Popo."

*The tall watch-tower where the sentry stood*

The old man started and looked down, his eyes searching the shadows below the palisades.

"Popo, it's us," Rata said. "Rata and Hine."

Popo let out his breath and wiped his hand across his forehead.

"You naughty children," he said. "What are you doing there?"

Rata climbed the ladder and stood by his side. "Well?"

"Please, Popo," Rata said softly, "we came out because we wanted to see the men in the canoes. We have never seen them at night."

"As you are here, you might as well stay," Popo answered.

Rata leaned over the side, "Come on up, Hine," he said. "Popo says we can stay here."

In a moment Hine was by his side. The children held tightly on to the rail of the watch-tower and looked down at the harbour. There were three lights which bobbed up and down in the water and they could hear the voices of the men in the canoes.

After looking carefully round him, Popo stood behind them and put his hands on their shoulders.

"You came just in time, children," he said. "You can't see very much from here, for I have often watched. The torches on the canoes look like glow-worms. The men must have had good hunting, for they have stayed in the same place all night."

"Why does that mean good hunting, Popo?"

"Well, you see, it shows that there have been plenty of fish. They have swum towards the lighted torches, and your father and the other men have been busy spearing them. If the fishing had not been good, they would have taken the canoes to other parts of the harbour."

"I love to see the lights," Hine said. "The water looks so dark and cold at night. When you see lights and hear the sound of voices it is much more comfortable."

Popo chuckled. "Sometimes I feel like that too, Hine, as I stand up here in

31

the darkness. But all the time you know that friends are below in the whares. They are asleep, but if danger comes, they will come as soon as I call out. And then, when the night is so black that you cannot even see the trees, slowly the sky grows lighter. Look!"

They all turned towards the east. Slowly, slowly the sky turned from black to grey. Then there was a pink flush, like the embers of a fire, on the clouds. It grew brighter, until a rim of golden fire crept over the horizon, and the sun began its long journey across the sky. Another day had dawned.

"You had better hurry back to the whare before you are missed," Popo said. "Tonight I will tell you the story of how light came into the world long, long ago, before there were any boys and girls living here."

And this is the story he told.

\* \* \*

Once upon a time, before there was night or day, Rangi, the Sky Father, held Papa, the Earth Mother, tightly. Their children, who were gods, could not see properly in the twilight. They had to crawl on their hands and knees, because there was not enough room for them to stand up.

Long years passed, and the children of Rangi and Papa were pale and bent. They longed for wind to blow over the hill tops, and light to warm them. At last they met together.

"What shall we do ?" they said. "We are not babies who need to be nursed by their mother. We are grown up now. We need room to move about in the world."

Then Tane, who was the strongest of them all, said, "Let us throw the Sky far away. Then it will be light, and we can live close to the Earth Mother."

The others all said yes, all except Tawhiri, the Wind God, who was especially fond of his father.

"You are very foolish," he said fiercely. "We are safe here, between our mother and father."

The others shouted him down. "We must have light."

They thrust Tawhiri aside. Rongo, the god of food, pressed his shoulders against the Sky Father and tried to push him away. He pushed and pushed but he could not move the sky. In the end he had to give in.

Tangaroa, the god of the fishes, tried next, but he could do no better. One after another, the gods pushed, but not one of them could move the sky.

At last Tane, the god of the forest, of birds and insects, stood up. He stood firmly on the earth and pressed his hands against the sky. Then he braced himself and took a deep breath. The Sky Father moved a little, and the air between earth and sky moaned as Tawhiri shouted angrily.

Rangi's arms loosed their grip on Papa. Tane heaved again, the sky was thrown away, farther and farther, so that the light flooded in, just as it does every morning when the sun peeps over the rim of the world. Up and up Rangi went, until his children could no longer see his face.

The gods looked around, and for the first time they could see the Earth Mother properly. A silver veil hung over her shoulders, and tear drops fell on her as Papa wept, but the gods were glad, because now they could move about and enjoy all the loveliness of earth and sky for the first time.

Now, although he had thrown the sky so far away from the earth, Tane loved his mother and father, and he longed to make them beautiful. His first gift was for his mother. The trees were his children, and he decided to plant them over the earth to keep her warm. The trees were his children, but Tane was still like a child himself. He had many things to learn. At first he made a mistake and planted them upside-down, so that their roots waved in the wind, and their leaves were pressed against the ground.

He was puzzled, because there was no place for his other children, birds and insects, to live amongst the roots. Then he saw what was wrong, and he turned them over. Their roots went down into the soil and held on firmly, while the leaves rustled in the breeze, and the birds made their home in the branches.

The Earth Mother looked beautiful in the soft light with her waving garment of green trees.

Tane looked up. Far above, Rangi lay still and grey, and the teardrops kept on falling down.

"I must make you beautiful too," Tane said.

He leaped up and put the red sun on the back of Rangi and the silver moon in front. They followed each other across the sky. When the sun shone down, the sky was blue

*Tane heaved again*

33

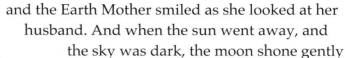and the Earth Mother smiled as she looked at her husband. And when the sun went away, and the sky was dark, the moon shone gently down on the hills and valleys.

But Tane had not finished his great work. From far away he brought a wonderful cloak which he spread right across the sky.

"No, it is too bright," the other gods cried, because it dazzled them. Tane rolled it back again, leaving only a little at the ends of the sky, where you may still see it at the rising and the setting of the sun.

*He turned them over*

"What else can I do to show my love for Rangi?" Tane asked.

"In the long, dark nights my heart still sorrows for Rangi," Papa replied. "I can see the shining moon on his breast, but it is not enough, for all the sky is dark."

Tane thought for a while. "I remember," he said. "On the great mountain at the very end of the world, the shining elves are at play. I will bring them for Rangi."

He travelled swiftly across the hills and plains, crossed rivers and endless seas, until he came to the place where there was neither land nor sea. On he went into the darkness, until far away he saw a glimmer of light. It was like the distant specks of light that you can see from the watch-tower, and you know that men are fishing in the harbour.

Tane felt glad, for he knew he was not alone in the darkness. Somewhere ahead of him was the great mountain where his brother Uru lived with his children, the Shining Ones. Uru lived on top of the mountain, and he welcomed Tane and asked news of their mother and father.

The two brothers sat on the veranda of the whare as they talked and watched the Shining Ones playing on the sand at the foot of the mountain.

"I saw the sky rolled back," Uru said. "I knew it was your work, my brother. Even from here you can see the far-off glow of light which shines between earth and sky. Long ago I escaped, so that my children could live

34

happily where there was room for them to play. Now our Mother Earth will be a happy place too, where living things can grow. Some day men and women will live amongst those trees which you have planted, Tane, and their children will swim in the great waves of the sea. They will grow the food of our brother Rongo, and take fish from Tangaroa. Surely your work is done, and now you may rest."

"Not yet, my brother," said Tane. "Rangi lies dark and still at night. I have fastened the moon on his breast, but it is not enough. Only one thing is needed. Will you give me some of your children to clothe him with living fire in the darkness of the night?"

Uru got up and walked backwards and forwards as he thought. "I love them," he said. "I thought they would keep me company here for ever. But perhaps you are right. You have made a place for them, Tane, and they would be happy with their grandfather."

He put his hands round his mouth and his voice rolled down the slopes of the mountain like thunder. The Shining Ones heard. They stopped their game and came rolling up the mountain to Uru.

As they came nearer, Tane saw them rolling over and over, for each Shining One was shaped like an eye. They glowed and twinkled, and the whole mountain was lit up as they came near.

Uru gave his brother a basket. Tane filled it with Shining Ones until the whole basket glowed with light. Uru tied it on to Tane's back, and the god of nature sped through the darkness towards his father.

Rangi saw him coming because of the light which spilled out of the basket. When Tane reached the sky, he took the basket from his back and fastened the Shining Ones on to his father's cloak. He hung a big light at each corner, and on the breast he placed five glowing lights in the form of a cross. The others he spread far and wide across the sky.

The basket in which he brought them still hangs there. It is the Milky Way. It is this soft light which still shelters the Shining Ones and protects the little children of light.

When the sun sank to rest that night, the stars began to twinkle brightly in the darkness. Tane lay on his back on the Earth Mother and watched his father shake out his robe until the whole sky was filled with the beauty of Rangi and the glory of the Shining Ones.

*The trees bent beneath the winds as Tawhiri threw them in front of him*

All would have ended well if it had not been for Tawhiri, the Wind God. He had gone to live with Rangi, preferring to keep away from his brothers.

When Tane made the sky beautiful, he hid from sight. He became angry as he saw the Earth Mother far below, and watched his brothers working and playing so peacefully in the light of the sun.

He saw Tane walking through the green forests, with birds flying round him and perching on his shoulders. He saw Tangaroa sleeping in the calm ocean while his fish-children swam round him.

"Ha ha," he laughed. "Now I will make trouble for my brothers."

He called the winds to him and held them in his hand. Then he swooped down from the sky, wrapped in storm clouds and flashing lightning. First he came to the land and rushed across it. The trees bent beneath the winds as Tawhiri threw them in front of him. Then he swept over the hills and down to the plains. Trees crashed to the ground, and when Tawhiri had gone, all the land was covered with broken trees and plants, and the voices of the birds were still.

On rushed the storm god and over the sea. Great waves rose and fell before the wind, and the surf thundered up the sandy beaches and crashed against the cliffs. Rocks and earth fell into the raging sea, and the gulls flew screaming upwards as they tried to escape from the wind and water. It was as though the sea was fighting against the land.

Tawhiri laughed louder as he saw how his brothers fought with each other. He swooped upwards, towards the sky. Gradually the waves died down, and the trees which had escaped the storm wind straightened themselves and spread their leaves in the sunshine again.

In the battle between Tane of the land and Tangaroa of the sea, the winner was really Tawhiri. He has never forgiven his brothers for what they did to the Sky Father. It was Tangaroa who turned the gods of land and sea into enemies.

Sometimes they remain at peace for a long time, but sooner or later the winds roar and Tangaroa hurls his waves against the land and tries to break it down and cover it with the cruel waves. So the old battle is fought all over again, until Tawhiri grows tired of his game and leaves them at peace once more.

But the sun shines more often than the wind blows. Tane has done all he can for the Sky Father, and he still does all he can for the Earth Mother. He made the trees put on their best flowers. Some of them he covered with berries, until all the forest were filled with singing birds as they looked for insects and honey and berries in the trees.

That is how the world was made, my children. When you look up into the blue sky and see the shining sun marching from east to west and feel his warmth on your bodies, remember that it was Tane who let light into the world. Remember that it was Tane who spread a blue cloak over the Sky Father and a green dress over the Earth Mother. Remember that it was Tane who put the sun up above to give us warmth and light in the daytime, and the moon to give her soft shining light in the night.

When the dark night is over and the dawn comes again to show us this lovely world of ours, remember that it was brought to you by Tane the Light Giver.

# THE BATTLE OF THE BIRDS

"LOOK at that one!" shouted Rata. "There he goes!"

They were watching the shags catching their morning meal of fish. There must have been a big shoal close to the shore, and Rata and Hine had been looking at the birds for some time. They flew up and then dived into the water.

"Sometimes they go so fast that you can't see them," Hine said. "There!"

She had heard the plunk! that Kawau the shag made as he entered the water. She counted slowly up to ten – "Ka tahi, Ka rua, Ka toru, Ka wha, Ka rima, Ka ono, Ka whitu, Ka waru, Ka iwa, ngahuru" – and as she said ngahuru, the shag bobbed out of the water with a shining fish in his beak.

"Funny things, shags," Rata said. "Look, some of them have come out to dry themselves."

On a rock a little way from the beach, three shags were perched. They stretched out their wings as they stood there, drying them in the sun.

After a while the children grew tired of watching them.

"What shall we play now?" Rata asked.

"I know," said Hine. "Let's see how many different kinds of birds we can see. I'll start off. Shag!"

"Listen!" replied Rata. "There's a flock of kakas coming."

They heard the noisy chattering of the birds as they flew over the tops of the trees. "That's one for me."

"Seagulls," Hine said. "Lots and lots of them. There are the little ones with red bills and the big black-backed ones. That makes three kinds for me."

"Tui," shouted Rata as the lovely song rang out and then got mixed up with funny clicks and chuckles. "And fantail," he added quickly, as he saw the fluttering little bird chasing insects close to them, snapping its beak.

"Penguins!" Hine squeaked with excitement. "Look. Over there."

They laughed to see the heads of the little blue birds bobbing in and out of the waves.

"Kuku," said Rata, as he saw the white breast and shining blue and green neck of a big wood pigeon, which sat on a branch close to them and said "Kuku" in a soft, dreamy voice.

"Four for me and four for you," Hine said. "Mine are all sea birds and yours are all birds of the forest. There are more sea birds than land birds."

"Oh no!" Rata said quickly. "Sea birds are no good – except Titi the shearwater," he added, licking his lips. "I've seen father spearing the pigeons, and he has sometimes let me help him with the snares."

"Sea birds are good," Hine said. "I shall go on counting them."

As they walked towards the pa along the curving beaches, and climbed the rocks that lay between each sheltered little bay, Rata kept close to the edge of the forest, shouting loudly whenever he saw a new kind of bird. Hine was not getting on nearly so well, but it was great fun when she looked over a rock to see a blue heron searching for crabs in a pool just below her. Catching sight of the little girl, he flapped slowly into the air, with his neck drawn in and his long legs trailing behind him.

"Ngahuru ma waru – eighteen," Rata said triumphantly after a while. "How many have you counted, Hine?"

"Ka iwa – nine," said Hine, "but sea birds are much harder to find."

"But they are important people," said a voice behind them.

"Popo, where did you come from?" the children shouted as they turned round and threw themselves at him.

"You were so busy that you didn't see old Popo walking behind you on the sand," said their friend. "You seemed very busy. What were you doing?"

"We were having a game," Hine said, "to see who could count the most birds. But it wasn't fair, was it, Popo?"

"Why not, my child?"

"I had only the sea birds but Rata chose the forest birds and there are far more of them."

*The battle of the birds*    page 46

Popo scratched his head and thought for a while. "I don't really know," he said at last. "There are many, very many birds of the sea, and if you count all those who wade on their long legs in the water and who fish in the streams and the swamps . . . well, I just don't know, Hine."

He stooped and lifted a heap of seaweed with the end of a flax stalk he was carrying, and watched the tiny little crabs scuttle across the sand as their hiding-place was taken away from them.

The children followed the old man as he led them over the hard wet sand, where the out-going tide had left little white flecks of foam, across the dry part of the beach where their feet sank deep into the soft sand, and sat down with their backs against the rough branch of a pohutukawa tree.

The children were quiet because they could see that Popo was ready to tell them a story. They burrowed their toes into the soft warm sand and looked up at the blue sky through the leaves of the tree. Popo snapped a dry twig in his hands. "Listen to the birds in the forest," he said at last. "Perhaps you are right, Hine. Perhaps there are more of them on the land. All day long we see the gulls fly past the pa, but that is because we are people of the sea as well as of the land; it is because we are fishermen that we have built our pa right beside the sea. Over there," he said with a sweep of his arm, "the land goes on, mountains and valleys and plains, grassland and swamp and forests which never seem to end. They are all full of birds. If we lived over there we should never see the ocean birds, except when the storm winds blew the gulls far inland.

"They know where to go, and where to find the food that suits them best, but it was not always so. Let me tell you a story."

\* \* \*

It happened a long, long time ago, when great Tane had thrown the Sky Father away from the earth and light came into the world. For long ages Tane was busy. He clothed the sky with clouds and stars, he fixed the sun and the moon in their places, he put the red cloak of the sunset

*Three shags were perched on a rock*

41

on his father's body.

And on Mother Earth he spread a cloak of green – trees and bushes, grass and rushes, until she looked more beautiful than the sky itself.

And then, when it was all finished, he made birds with swiftly beating wings, birds which sang and danced all day long, birds to spread the seeds of the trees so that the forest would never die. So it was that the Earth Mother's beautiful clothes were alive, and so it is that the garment covers her to this day.

When the birds were made, they did not know where to go, or what to eat, and Tane had to show them how to fill their hungry little stomachs. He clapped his hands, and when they came to him he showed them all the trees of the forest which had fruit and berries. There were the berries of the konini, puriri, matai, miro, kahikatea, maire, hinau, karaka – oh, and a hundred others. He showed them the ribbonwood and the kowhai, and many others. There were leaves which were good to eat, too.

"These are all good to eat," Tane said to the pigeon. To Kakariki, the parakeet, he said, "You can eat berries, and seeds as well – flax seeds, toetoe seeds."

To Kiwi with its long bill, he said, "There is good food for you in the ground – worms and snails, as well as berries."

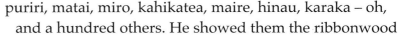
*He made birds*

To the fantail as it twisted and turned in the air, and fluttered its big fan, "You may eat the insects as they fly in the air."

To the tomtits he said, "Insects and grubs for you, my little ones, because you can see them with those sharp eyes of yours."

There were other birds which he took down to the sea-shore and showed them where they could find plenty to eat – crabs for the herons, insects and tiny shellfish for the stilts, fish and crabs for the penguins, scraps and fish of every kind for the gulls. "There is the sea for you," he said to the petrels, the mutton birds, the albatrosses, the skuas, the mollymawks, and the gannets. "It is full of fish, so that you never need go hungry."

Then he left them and went on with his work, and for a long time the birds were happy as they fed on the food that Tane had given them, and learned how to build nests for themselves and care for their chicks.

Insects and berries and leaves, honey and grubs, fish and crabs and snails, and every kind of sea food and forest food was theirs for the taking. Each bird knew its home and its time for going out and coming in, its song to sing and its food to eat. Those who had gone down to the sea played in the great waters or on the wet shining sands where land and water meet. The others stayed inland amongst the cool green shadows of the trees, where their voices made the forest ring with music. Some came out only at night and crept through the gloom, and pounced on their prey while the others slept.

One day, Kawau, the boasting river cormorant, visited Kawau, his cousin, the sea cormorant. He was surprised to see how far the ocean stretched towards the sunset and the wide spaces in which to fly.

"What sort of fish do you catch in the great waters?" he asked.

His cousin threw him a fish. "Try that," he said.

Kawau stretched out his long neck and caught the fish in his beak. He swallowed it whole in one gulp. But the fish had prickly spines which caught in his throat. Kawau cried out with pain.

"That is no good," he said scornfully. "You must come to my home and we will hunt the fat river eels together."

The months went by, and one day the sea cormorant paid a visit to his cousin. He left his home and flew up the river with slowly beating wings, until he heard a cry of welcome.

"It is you at last, sea cousin," the river cormorant cried. "Come down here and see my home."

The sea cormorant fluttered downwards and perched beside his cousin on the branch of a tree which stretched across a deep pool in the river, which lay in the shadow of the bush. Above their heads the leaves danced in the bright sunshine, but down below the water was black because the trees leaned over it.

"It is cold here," said the sea cormorant.

The river cormorant laughed harshly.

"There is better fishing in this river than on all the beaches from here to the place where the spirits begin their long journey

*The sea cormorant perched beside his cousin on the branch*

to the other world," he said. "Look, cousin! When your eyes are used to the darkness you will see two darker shadows in the pool."

The sea cormorant bent his head and tried to look into the dark water.

At first he could see nothing, but presently the water seemed to get clearer, and sure enough, there were two long, thin shapes swimming lazily close to the bank.

"What are they?" he asked.

"They are eels," was the reply. "Beautiful fat eels such as you never see in the wind-swept waters of your home. I will take the one over there, and you can have the one below us. We must not scare them away, so we will dive together.

"Be careful, cousin!"

They waited quietly, while the eels swam slowly through the water. "Now!" croaked the river cormorant, and, just as if they were one, the two birds plunged head first into the pool.

The eels flashed away into the shelter of their home under the bank, but they were too late. The strong beaks closed over their necks and a moment later they were lifted high into the air as the cormorants flew back to their perch.

The eels struggled with all their might, but the river cormorant threw back his head and the long fish slipped down his throat. The sea cormorant did the same.

He looked at his cousin.

"That was wonderful," he said. "No spines! No scales! Nothing but good fish! Cousin, I think I will come and live with you, for your food is much better than mine."

Then the river cormorant was sorry that he had boasted of his rich river food.

"This is not your home," he said quickly. "You would not be happy here."

"I think I would," said the sea cormorant. "There is plenty of food for both of us."

"You are like all the sea birds; you have no manners. Get away back to the sea," the river cormorant said angrily.

He flew at his cousin and drove him away.

The sea cormorant did not stay to argue. He flew as fast as he could away from his cousin, but when he got back to the beach, he stood on a high rock and called loudly, "Come and listen to what I have to say. I have something important to tell you."

The great albatrosses came floating in from the sea, the oystercatchers and the gulls and the terns gathered round him until, as far as one could see, the water was covered with floating birds.

"Listen," he shouted. "I have been far inland to visit my cousin, the river cormorant, and a wonderful thing happened. In the river where the water is fresh, there are wonderful fish which my cousin calls eels. They are good to eat. They are long and fat and have hardly any bones. When you eat them they slip easily down your throat."

"And what has that got to do with us?" a great albatross said.

"I'll tell you what it has to do with us," the cormorant said. "Why should we have sore throats because the sea fish are hard to eat? It isn't fair. All we have to do is fly inland together and drive all the forest birds away, and then we can live on lovely fat juicy eels. They can come down to the sea and find out what it is like to be a sea bird."

"It seems a silly idea," grumbled the old albatross, "but perhaps it would be a nice change. Come on," and his great strong wings began to beat and the other birds made way for him. Faster, faster he went, until a wave came in and lifted him up, so that he flew above the water. Up and up he went, in huge circles, and the other birds followed him, until the sky seemed full of their beating wings. When they were all in the air they turned and began to fly up the river.

Far away, above the peaceful pool in the river, the river cormorant was telling his friends about his cousin's visit.

"You were foolish to be so boastful," said a fierce kingfisher. "Why did you say anything?"

"Yes, I can see I was foolish," said Kawau. "But that is in the past, and we cannot live the past again. What we have to think about is the future. I am afraid that my cousin will come back and bring his friends with him. We must be ready for them."

Just then, Pitoitoi, the robin, fluttered down crying. "They're coming! I can hear them already. The sound of their wings is like the thunder of waves on the beach."

Kawau danced on his perch with excitement. "Who'll be the scout?" he shouted. "Who'll see when they are coming?"

"I'll be the scout," said Koekoea, the cuckoo. "I'll see when they are coming."

He flew up above the trees, and presently he called out his warning – "*Koo-o-o-e!*"

The waiting birds heard his cry, and then, far away, another call, "*A-ha!*" as Karoro the gull called out a challenge.

"Who'll answer the battle cry?" asked Kawau.

"I," said Fantail. "I'll flaunt a challenge with my fan."

"Who'll sing the battle song?" asked Kawau.

"I," said Tui. "Let Honge, the crow, and Tiraueke the saddleback, and Wharauroa the short-tailed cuckoo, and Kereru the pigeon help me, and I'll lead the battle song."

When the song was ended, Kawau faced the angry birds.

"Who'll begin the fight?" he cried.

"I'll begin the fight," shouted Ruru the owl. "With my beak and claws I'll begin the fight."

He rose from his perch and swooped down on the sea birds, with the land birds flying in a great crowd behind him.

It was a long and fierce battle, when feathers fell like snow-flakes, and the sun rose high in the heavens.

At first the sea birds attacked in their thousands, but after a while they grew frightened. The land birds fought more fiercely, until the sea birds were driven back. They turned tail and flew back to their homes in terror.

"*Ke-ke-ke-ke!*" laughed Parera the duck as the gulls flew down the river like a cloud in the wind.

\* \* \*

"And so the battle ended," said Popo. "That is why the sea birds do not eat the land birds' food. And so there is peace between them in this lovely world that Tane made for us, long, long ago."

46

# How Uenuku became a Rainbow

RATA sat up and rubbed the sleep out of his eyes. It was dark inside the sleeping house, but he could tell that it was early morning because the door was open. The world outside looked like a panel of woolly whiteness. He felt with his hands until he found his kilt and wrapped it round his middle. When he got to the door and looked out, he could see nothing but grey mist which felt damp against his skin. Somewhere a seagull cried, and the waves were lapping against the rocky sides of the pa. Presently he could see the tutu trees on the far side of the marae. It was like looking at seaweed under water. Their trunks were hidden by broad bands of mist, but where the fog was thinner he could see their tops.

He walked across and nearly fell over something soft and warm. "Be careful where you're going," a voice grumbled sleepily. Rata bent down and saw that it was Popo.

"Hullo, Popo. What are you doing here?"

Popo held up the blade of his greenstone axe, and Rata smiled.

"Couldn't you sleep last night?" he asked.

"No."

Rata knew that when the old man could not sleep, he would sit up and rub his precious axe on his fat stomach, round and round, until at last he fell asleep. If he woke up during the night, he would keep on rubbing it until he dropped off again. "You've been polishing it for *months*, Popo. When will it be finished?" Popo rubbed his fingers over the smooth stone and thought for a while. "Maybe when Puanga rises in the new year, maybe it will be ready then. It will be a good axe."

47

Rata reached up and pulled off a spray of berries. Popo smacked his arm. "Leave those berries alone, you naughty boy," he said. "You know they are poisonous."

"Yes, I know," Rata said, and pretended to swallow them.

Popo snatched them out of his hand and threw them into the grass.

"You'll come to a bad end!" he said fiercely, but Rata only smiled at him. "Do you know what happens to little children who get tutu poisoning? Do you?"

"No, Popo."

"'There's only one cure. They have to be shaken over a fire of green leaves and branches until the poison goes out of them. You listen to old Popo! It was done to me when I was a boy, and believe me, little Rata, the cure is worse than the poison!"

"Did you die, Popo?"

The fat man pulled the boy's ear until Rata cried, "All right, Popo. I wasn't going to eat the berries. Hasn't Hine come out yet?"

"No, I haven't seen her this morning. But there's been nothing to see out here in the fog. My ears have been my eyes, Rata, and I've heard feet pattering. Maybe the fairies have been here, but I stayed still and they never saw me."

Rata shivered and crept closer to his friend.

"I am Uenuku – tell me your name"

"Listen!" he whispered. There was a faint sound among the trees, like twigs snapping. They both listened. Something was brushing through the leaves. There was silence for a little while, followed by the patter of bare feet.

"Come over here, Hine," Popo called. "I know your steps."

Hine came over to them and sat down, shaking the silver mist out of her hair.

"It was on a morning like this that the Rainbow Man found the Mist Girl," Popo said, putting his arm round her.

48

Uenuku looked at the mist over the lake. It had been thick in the forest but here it stood up like the trunk of a tall tree. Two young women were swimming in the lake. He could see that they were beautiful even through the mist which was wrapped round them like a cloud. Further out the air was clear, but near the shore everything had turned to silver. The bathers were the Mist Girl and her sister the Misty Rain Girl. They had come down from the sky to swim in the clear lake water.

Uenuku knelt down at the water's edge and said to the Mist Girl,

"I am Uenuku. Tell me your name."

"I am Hine, the Girl of the Mist."

Uenuku stretched out his arms. "Come and live with me in this world of light," he said. "I have never seen a woman so beautiful as you. I am strong and will take care of you."

"I cannot leave my home," the Mist Girl replied. "My sister is waiting for me to go back with her."

"You will love this world," Uenuku pleaded. "It is not cold and empty like the sky. Come with me, Girl of the Mist."

She took a step towards him and then drew back. "You would not be happy with me," she said.

"I would always love you," Uenuku said.

"But you do not understand, Uenuku. I come from the sky, and though I might spend the night with you, I should have to go back to my home as soon as the sky grew light."

"I still want you. Even though I shall be lonely during the day, please come and live with me."

The Mist Girl smiled. "I will come with you," she said.

The next morning, before the sun had risen, the Mist Girl met her sister. They seemed to drift together like clouds up and up into the blue sky. Every morning the Mist Girl disappeared, and every night she came back to earth to be with her husband. But Uenuku was lonely in the daytime and wished that Hine would stay with him all the time.

One day he tied mats across the windows and pushed moss into the crevices between the planks. When the door was shut the whare was as dark as night. Early the next morning the Rain Girl called her sister.

49

"Come, Hine, we must go up into the sky now."

"I am coming," the Mist Girl answered.

"Where are you going?" Uenuku asked.

"It is time for me to go."

"Nonsense," he replied, pretending to be half-asleep. "Why are you disturbing me? Look around you. There is no light anywhere."

"But morning must be near. My sister has called me."

"Your sister has made a mistake. Perhaps she has seen the moonlight or the starlight. There is no light anywhere. Go to sleep again."

Hine lay down. "She must be mistaken," she said, "but it is strange. I do not understand it. She has never made such a mistake before."

The Misty Rain Girl kept on calling, and her voice mingled with the sound of the waking birds, but Uenuku kept on saying she was mistaken. Presently she could wait no longer, and the husband and wife heard her voice growing fainter as she left them.

"I am sure there is something wrong," the Mist Girl said, suddenly wide awake. "Listen, I can hear the birds singing."

They listened. The Rain Girl had gone, but the song of the birds was very loud and there were voices outside. The Mist Girl ran to the door, forgetting her cloak. She pulled the door wide open, and sunshine filled the whare. She stood there a moment, and a gasp of amazement went up from the people, for the Mist Girl was so slender and beautiful that no one had ever seen anyone so wonderful before. She did not look as though she belonged to the earth.

Uenuku followed her out, smiling at the way everyone was admiring his wife. As he passed through the doorway, Hine sprang on to the roof of the house and climbed up to the ridgepole. Her long hair covered her body. She began to sing. It was a sad song; there was pain in it, and longing; and love for Uenuku. Then a strange thing happened.

Out of a clear sky a tiny cloud drifted down. It rolled itself round

*The Rain Girl kept on calling*

50

*The cloud rolled itself round her, fold on fold*

her, fold on fold, until she could no longer be seen. Only her voice could be heard, coming from the tiny cloud. Then the song stopped and the cloud drifted away from the roof. It rose upwards, higher and higher, until it seemed to dissolve in the bright sunshine.

Poor Uenuku was heart-broken. Night after night he waited for his Mist Girl, but she never came back. One day he left his home and set out on a long search for her. He met with many adventures and passed through strange countries, but no one could tell him what had happened to the Mist Girl.

As his search went on, year after year, he grew old and bent and toothless, and at last, lonely and disappointed, he died in a far-away country. Then the kind gods took pity on him. They lifted up his old body and changed him into a rainbow and put him in the sky where everyone could see him.

\* \* \*

While Popo had been talking the mist had grown thin and drifted away. They could see right across the pa. The sun was sparkling on the sea, but there was still a cloud of mist lying above the island in the harbour, and the broken bow of a rainbow rested above it.

"Look," Popo said, "there is the Rainbow Man!"

"He has found his wife at last," Hine said, and her eyes were shining.

Popo pulled her hair playfully, and the three of them went across to the cooking-sheds to see whether breakfast was ready.

52

# MAUI LOOKS FOR FIRE

RATA straightened his back and sighed. Hine giggled.

"I told you so," she said.

"It was only because you didn't hold your foot still," he said crossly.

The children had been playing on the far side of the court yard, under the trees by the big fence.

Rata had said that he could make fire. They had hunted about until they found two pieces of wood which looked like the ones that the grown-ups used. They had put a flat piece on the ground and Hine held it down with her foot while Rata rubbed a pointed stick backwards and forwards along it. He had rubbed until his back ached but he could not get even a wisp of smoke to come from it.

A shadow fell across them and when they looked up, their old friend Popo was standing there.

"What are you doing, children?" he asked. Rata looked sulky and said nothing, so Hine answered for him.

"We have been trying to make fire with these two pieces of wood, but something seems to have gone wrong. Perhaps it is because we don't know the magic spells?"

Popo squatted down on his heels, picked up the pieces of wood and looked at them closely.

"No," he said at last. "Fire can be made without magic. Listen carefully, and I will tell you how men learned the secret of fire. And then perhaps we will

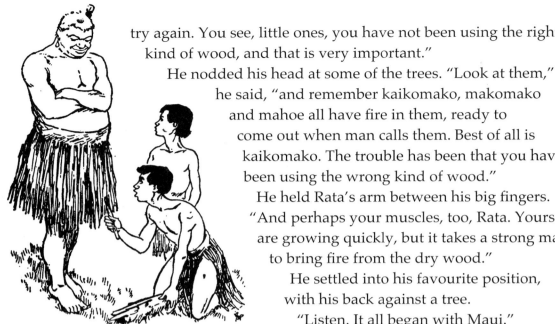

try again. You see, little ones, you have not been using the right kind of wood, and that is very important."

He nodded his head at some of the trees. "Look at them," he said, "and remember kaikomako, makomako and mahoe all have fire in them, ready to come out when man calls them. Best of all is kaikomako. The trouble has been that you have been using the wrong kind of wood."

He held Rata's arm between his big fingers. "And perhaps your muscles, too, Rata. Yours are growing quickly, but it takes a strong man to bring fire from the dry wood."

He settled into his favourite position, with his back against a tree.

"Listen. It all began with Maui."

*"We have been trying to make fire"*

* * *

Maui was at home with his brothers. They had been singing inside the house and now everyone was tired, and very quiet, before the time of sleep. Maui had been watching the fires on the big fat stones on the floor until only the red embers were left. Blue flames flickered over them.

"Where does the fire come from?" he asked suddenly.

His brothers were tired of his questions. He was such a restless boy, always asking silly questions.

"It is here," one of them said impatiently. "Why do you want to know where it comes from?"

"It must have come from somewhere," Maui said stubbornly.

"So long as it is here for us to use, why do we need to know how it came to us?"

Maui thought for a moment, and said, "What happens if it goes out?"

"We make sure that it never goes out."

"But what if it did go out? Where would we get more from?"

"If you really must know, Maui, our mother would get it for us, or she would send one of the slaves. She knows where it comes from. We don't want to know, because it is hard to get and very dangerous."

Maui could not go to sleep for thinking about the fire. When everyone was asleep he got up very quietly. He took a calabash of water and poured it carefully on to the embers. At first they sizzled and spluttered. Steam rose and white ashes flew out, but as he went on pouring, the embers went black until at last the fire was dead.

During the night it grew cold. An old man got up to put more wood on the fire. When he found that it was out he cried, "Aue! Aue! The fire has gone. We shall die of cold!"

His voice woke the others, and everyone began to talk at once. The brothers' voices were loudest of all.

"This is Maui's fault," they shouted. "Why should we put up with him any longer, Mother? There has been nothing but trouble since he came here."

*"The fire has gone!"*

"Where are you, Maui-tikitiki?" his mother asked, and in the darkness Maui replied, "I am here, Mother Taranga."

"Why did you do such a silly thing? The way into the underworld is long and dark and there are many perils for my slaves to face when they bring back fire."

Maui groped in the darkness until he felt his mother's arm and squeezed it.

"I will go," he said. "I put out the fire because I need to know where the fire comes from. Let the slaves lie down again. Tell me where I may find fire in the land of shadows. Who is the keeper of fire?"

"Yes, it is right that you should go, Maui," Taranga replied. "Perhaps it will cure you of your tricks. You will have to be careful that you don't get into trouble. I will tell you how to go through the land of shadows until you come to the place where the grandmother of your grandmother lives. She is very old but she is strong and will not stand any nonsense. She looks after the fire of the underworld. If she asks your name, tell her who you are. You must be careful, and very polite. If you try to deceive her, she will punish you."

55

Taranga went with Maui to the door. They stood in the moonlight while she pointed out the way he must take. Maui listened and grinned as he set out on his journey to the land of shadows.

Presently he lost sight of the moon. The path went downwards and it grew darker and darker. He had to put his hands in front of him to feel his way. He seemed to hear strange noises, and unseen things brushed against his face in the darkness, but he went steadily downwards.

At last he saw a tiny flickering light in the distance. As he stumbled on, it grew larger and larger until he could see that there was a house with firelight shining from the door and window. He came close to it and he could see that it was covered with wonderful carvings. Fire seemed to shoot out of the eyes of the big carved figures and he felt waves of heat coming from the doorway.

A woman's voice, old and sounding like the crackling of a stick in the fire, came from the house.

"Who is the bold mortal who stares at the house of Mahuika of the Fire? Do you come from the east?"

"No, grandmother."

"From the west?"

"No."

"From the south?"

"No."

"Do you come from where the wind blows from?"

"Yes. It is Maui, grandmother's grandmother."

"I have five great-great-grandchildren called Maui. Are you Maui the youngest?"

"Yes, I am Maui-tikitiki-a-Taranga."

The old woman chuckled. "I knew it," she said. "It couldn't be any other Maui. What do you want from your grandmother, Maui-the-last-one?"

"I want to take fire back to my mother and brothers, for the hearth-fire has gone out at home."

"I can give you fire, Maui," said Mahuika. She pulled out one of her finger-nails and it burst into flame.

"Carry it carefully, Maui, and light your fires with it."

Maui wrapped it in moss so that it smouldered and, saying good-bye to his great-great-grandmother, he went away. When he was out of sight he threw

*The fire followed Maui, roaring as it went*    page 57

it on the ground and stamped on it until the fire was out. He went back to the whare of Mahuika.

"Who is it now?" the old lady called out.

"It is Maui again."

"What do you want this time?"

"I want more fire. The fire went out as I was carrying it."

Mahuika scowled at him.

"You did not listen to my words, great-great-grandchild. You have been careless. I will give you another finger-nail, but you must hold your hand round the flame so that the wind cannot blow it out."

Maui took it away, holding it carefully, but when she could no longer see him he put it out and went back for more. Every time he was given a flaming finger-nail he did the same. Every time he went back he was given yet another, and Mahuika grew more and more angry.

When Maui came back for the eleventh time and Mahuika had given him all her finger-nails she was furious with him.

"You are trying my patience too far. This is your last chance, little man-child."

She gave him one of her toe-nails, but Maui only grinned at her impishly and presently came back for another, and another, and another. And then only one toe-nail remained. Mahuika heard him coming. She stood up, the ground rumbled and the walls of the house shook. Long tongues of flame burst through the windows of the whare. Maui put his arm in front of his eyes to shield them from the heat and struggled through the door. Clouds of smoke swirled round inside but he could see the angry flames in Mahuika's eyes.

"Great-great-grandmother," he began; but his voice was drowned by her voice. She took off the tenth toe-nail and threw it at the young man.

It fell on the ground at his feet and burst into flame. There was a noise like thunder and the fire jumped up at him like a dog. Maui turned round and ran outside. The fire followed him, roaring as it went. He could see every stone and tree as he ran, for the fire had lit up every part of the underworld. The faster Maui ran the faster the flames travelled. They licked his back and the perspiration poured down his face.

Then he remembered a spell that Tama had taught him when he was a little boy. He repeated it quickly and turned into a bush hawk. For a little while he gained on the fire as he beat his powerful wings, but soon the fire caught up with him again. Showers of sparks flew around him and the heat singed his feathers so much that to this very day the hawk is brown as if he has passed through the fire.

In another moment he would have been burnt, but he remembered a different spell of Tama's. Below there was a pool of water. Maui folded his wings and, in the shape of a fish, slipped into the pool whose clear water closed over him. He lay on the bottom and looked up at the raging flames through the clear water. Then steam drifted over the surface so that he could no longer see. Even in the depths the water grew hot . . . and still hotter, until in some parts it was boiling. Before it was too late he sprang out and raced on, out of the world of shadows into the bright sunshine. The forest burst into flame and the smoke darkened the sky.

It seemed as though the whole world might catch on fire. At this terrible time Maui remembered Tama and the gods who protected his old friend. He sent a prayer to them and they heard him, and saw that the world was in peril. They sent rain, heavy rain which poured on to the flame and broke through the walls of fire.

Maui turned round and watched. He could not feel the heat, and the flames were growing small and feeble. A harsh cry came from the fire. Mahuika was in the middle of it. She felt the cold rain beating on her and driving her down to the ground where the water was swirling. She ran back quickly to the underworld. To save her precious fire, she threw it into the last of the trees she passed – into kaikomako, mahoe and makomako.

Maui went on till he reached his own village. His brothers were waiting for him, and they seemed as angry as Mahuika had been. Their eyes were red from the smoke of the forest fire and their cloaks were wet with the rain that had fallen. Their feet squelched in the soft mud.

"Maui," they cried as soon as they saw him. "What have you done now! We are burnt in the fire and drowned in the rain, and now we have lost fire for ever. Mahuika will never give it to us again. We will shiver in the cold at night, and in the day-time we must eat our food raw."

Maui snapped his fingers in their faces.

"I have brought you fire which will last for ever. Look!"

He broke off a dry branch from a kaikomako tree and with a greenstone adze formed it into two pieces of wood which he rubbed together. Presently a wisp of smoke curled upwards and a tiny tongue of flame followed. Maui fanned it into a blaze and lit the fire on the hearth-stone.

"We shall never need to go to Mahuika again for fire," he said to his silent brothers. "It is hidden in the kaikomako, the mahoe, and the makomako, for ever and ever. If the rains come and the fire goes out, there it will be, waiting for us and ready to do our bidding like a slave."

* * *

Popo got up and went inside his whare, returning presently with two pieces of wood. "The fire is hidden here, for this is kaikomako wood."

He put one piece on the ground. It was as long as his arm from elbow to wrist and down the middle was a shallow groove.

"See, I will raise one end with this stone. Put your foot on the other end,

*She threw her fire into the last of the trees*

59

Hine, and keep it steady."

He kneeled down facing Hine, and took a rubbing stick in his hands, with his thumbs underneath and his palms on top. He began to rub the round point up and down the groove, gently at first, but pressing harder and harder as he went on.

After a while a little dust had collected in the groove and there was a smell of burning wood. Popo stopped and gathered it together in a little heap at the end of the groove. He rubbed harder than ever. Beads of perspiration formed on his forehead and ran down into his eyes, but he only shook his head and kept on rubbing. The groove on the bottom stick grew darker in colour. The children saw a tiny thread of smoke curling up from the wood. "Faster, faster," said Popo, as the rubbing stick flew up and down and Hine had to press with all her strength to keep the bottom piece still.

The dried powder glowed redder and redder, and grew bigger, while smoke began to pour from it.

"The work is nearly done," said Popo. "Fire is living in the groove. You can take your foot off now, Hine."

He put down the rubbing stick, emptied the burning powder on to some dried cabbage-tree leaves, and waved them in the air.

"There you are," he said as the leaves burned in the still air. "That is how you make fire. But remember, little ones, that it is the gift which Maui won from Mahuika when the world was young and different from what it is today."

"Thank you, Popo," Hine said. "We will remember this. Some day when Rata has grown into a man, he will be able to do it as well as you."

"Tell us, Popo," Rata said. "Where did Mahuika get the fire from?"

Popo put his head back and roared with laughter.

"You are as bad as Maui," he said. "Well, I suppose it is a good thing to be curious. See what came of Maui's curiosity! But I can't tell you the answer to that question, Rata. Ask your father some time. He is a wise man, much wiser than old Popo who is only fit for telling stories for little girls and boys."

Hine put her hand into the old man's and smiled up at him. "I think you tell the most wonderful stories in the world, Popo," she said.

"Bless you," the old man said. He patted her head, gathered up his sticks and went inside.

"I'm going to ask Father where fire really came from tonight," Rata told her, and so he did.

Father looked into the fire for a long time before he answered.

"It is a wise question, Rata. When you get older you will find that children ask questions which even the wisest men cannot answer. I can only tell you what I think.

"Remember that Mahuika lived in the underworld, somewhere far under this world of ours. It is a world of shadows, but also of fire. Far away in the middle of the big island on which we live there is a place where fire lives under the ground. I have seen this strange thing with my own eyes. And to the south are great mountains which sometimes throw out burning rocks which set the forest on fire.

"Perhaps it is this fire that Mahuika found long ago and gave to Maui. Perhaps it was he who found that fire lives in the wood and is brought to life when it is rubbed. But best of all is to remember that fire is man's slave, to do his bidding and to come to life when he calls it."

\* \* \*

"Father knows more than Popo," Rata whispered to Hine as she pulled the mat over him.

"Yes," she replied, "but I liked Popo's story best."

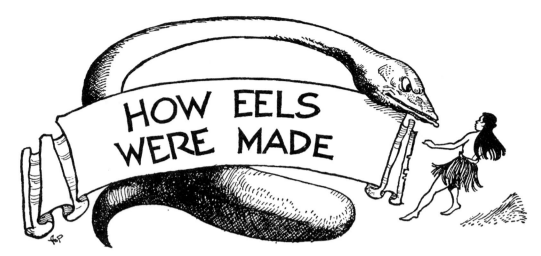

# HOW EELS WERE MADE

THE early morning air was cold as Rata and Hine went along the forest track that led to the inner harbour. Through the trees they could see the waves breaking on the rocks below, and the little gold and silver beaches where they sometimes loved to play.

The path came out on to the beach where a pohutukawa tree sprawled over the sand. They climbed over its broad trunk, past the rock in which the sea had worn a hole, past the last steep climb over the rocks, and on to the beach at the very end of the harbour.

A stream flowed across the sand. They paddled up it, and through the bush, until they came to a pool where there was good fishing for eels. The children felt that it was just the right sort of day to play by the pool, ending with a tasty morsel of cooked eel at night.

Rata threw off his short grass kilt and jumped into the water. The sun was shining and the water seemed icy cold on his warm body at first, but he soon got used to it. He swam slowly round the edge, feeling under the banks until his fingers closed over the slippery body of an eel. It wriggled out, but Rata caught it with his other hand and brought it to the surface. He sank his strong white teeth into its slimy body. Holding the wriggling fish in his mouth, he swam across the pool and threw it up to Hine, who pushed it into the small basket she had brought with her.

"Let's go up to the eel weir," Rata suggested, and leaving the basket in a cool place, they went upstream to where the top of the weir posts showed above the water.

While Rata lay sunning himself on the grass, Hine crawled along the fence of the weir, hanging on to the posts and dragging herself along the manuka brushwood which let the water through but guided the eels downstream to the big eelpot that had been tied between the two walls.

Presently she reached the place where the walls came together. The river raced through the narrow opening, but the water was clear, and as she peered down at the eelpot she noticed that the guiding net had been torn. Perhaps it had been broken by a drifting log, for the stream must have been high during the storm a few nights ago.

Hine shifted her position so that she could see more clearly, but the manuka branch on which she was leaning snapped in two, and she plunged headfirst into the water. She was not frightened for she could swim like a fish, but as she turned to come to the surface a sudden pang of fear shot through her.

The force of the current had swept her against the brushwood, so that it was difficult to move. She caught hold of the crosspieces on the fence and began to pull herself up, but her foot had caught in a crevice between the heavy ends of the manuka sticks. No matter how much she struggled, she could not work it loose, and a bubbling cry came from her lips.

Rata had been watching her from the bank. When she lost her hold and tumbled into the stream he fell over on his back shouting with laughter. When he looked again, he expected to see his sister climbing out. But there was no sign of her and Rata knew that something had gone wrong. He raced along the narrow fence at a speed he would never have dared at any other time and looked down into the water where Hine had disappeared. He saw her pressed against the brushwood, not moving as the water raced past her. He slipped into the stream, gasping as the water swept him against the fence. He turned his face to it and dragged himself down by the crosspieces, holding his breath. He caught Hine's arm and pulled, but she did not move.

Then he realised that her foot was caught; holding his breath and working desperately under the pressure of water, he felt round with his hands and discovered the pieces of wood that had sprung together and caught her foot.

He held them apart and worked her foot loose. Hine slid down to the bed of the stream, but Rata caught her by the hair. His lungs felt as though they were bursting, but he pulled her up slowly until at last he reached the top. He slipped his arm round her shoulders and held her head above water while he struggled to get the air into his lungs again.

Hine lay lifeless against the manuka brush. Still holding her tightly, Rata worked his way from post to post until he reached the bank. It was a big struggle for the boy to get his sister on to the bank, but at last he managed it and laid her face-downwards on the grass. The water ran from her nose and mouth and Rata rubbed her hands, not knowing what to do.

*He had a big struggle to get his sister to the bank*

Presently she moved a little, but she could not speak. The sun dried her back and after a long time she sat up and said, "What has happened, Rata?"

"Don't you remember?" said Rata, smiling so that she wouldn't feel frightened. "You fell into the water, but you're all right now."

Hine pushed her hair back from her face. "Yes, l remember," she said. "Oh, Rata, I was so frightened. Did you get me out?"

Rata felt silly and kicked a piece of wood with his bare toe. "lt wasn't anything," he said. "Do you feel all right now? I think we'd better go home."

They set off together and came to the tiny waterfall where a side stream entered the river. A shelf of rock covered with moss and creepers overhung the fall, and Rata peered up under it.

"It's still there," he said.

"What?"

"The enchanted stone."

"Who told you it was there?"

"Popo."

"What's it for?"

"To bring plenty of eels to the weir, silly."

Rata grinned suddenly. "I think it must be a very good charm," he said. "It mistook you for a big fat eel, Hine, and it tried its best to catch you."

"Who tried to catch you?" asked a voice they knew. They turned round and saw Popo standing behind them. He had a bird spear in his hand and he was carrying three fat wood pigeons, their lovely breasts shining in the sunlight.

"Who tried to catch my Hine?" he repeated, and she told him what had happened.

"That's a brave boy," said Popo approvingly. "I must tell your father about this. You are your father's son. But now we must go home, because Hine must rest this afternoon. I'll tell you a story as we go, and then the way won't seem so long. What sort of a story do you want today?"

"Tell us one about eels, Popo."

The fat man rubbed his chin thoughtfully. "I should have thought you had had enough eels for one day. But if you really want one, I can tell you the story of the father of eels. Come on. We'll walk slowly and then you can listen as we go."

\* \* \*

*Popo had three fat wood pigeons*

Tuna-roa was the father of eels. He was a big fellow. My word, he was a big eel! Even his name meant Long Eel. He lived in a swamp on the back of this great fish that Maui pulled out of the sea. You remember how Maui caught his fish, don't you? Afterwards Maui lived on this great island with his wife Hina.

Every day Hina went down to the

65

swamp to fill her calabash with water. One morning, as she bent over to dip it in, there was a great swirl in the water, and Tuna-roa shot up above the surface.

* * *

"There's the basket," Rata interrupted, and darted over to get it. "Have a look, Popo."

Popo raised the side and looked at the eel. "Yes, that's a fine eel. You must let me have a piece of him tonight."

He closed the basket and gave it to Rata who held it by the handle and slung it over his shoulder. "Go on, Popo."

* * *

The water dripped from Tuna-roa as he held his head high in the air. Hina was frightened and she turned and started to run, but she was too late. Tuna's tail swung round and struck her between the shoulders so that she fell forward on her face.

Hina did not tell her husband what had happened, but the next morning she kept watch at the pool. She saw Tuna gliding along under the water, and ran away quickly, but her foot turned on a stone. Tuna again caught her a crushing blow with his great tail.

This time Hina told her husband. Maui was angry. He went into the forest and cast spells on the trees to make them do his will. Then he cut them down and made them into tools. He made spades that would dig fast and deep with no one to hold them, spears that would sink easily into flesh, and knives with sharp cutting edges. Then he took all these tools to the swamp and set them to work.

The spades dug a broad ditch which stretched from the swamp right down to the sea. Maui stretched a net across the ditch and sat down to wait. Presently the rain fell. The little stream poured into the swamp. The water rose and rose until it reached the ditch. It burst the narrow barrier of earth that the spades had left and roared down the trench. It carried great lumps of earth with it, tree-trunks and boulders, and right in the middle of it was Tuna-roa.

He struggled and shouted, but it was no use. The water swept him straight

*With one blow he cut off Tuna's head*

into the net. Maui was sitting waiting for him. He raised his sharpest knife and with one blow he cut off Tuna's head. The water rolled it down the trench, and right out to sea. Then Maui cut off Tuna's tail and, in his rage, chopped his body up into little bits.

But that was not the end of Tuna-roa, my children. Did I not say that Tuna-roa was the father of eels? And would I tell you a lie? Maui went home, but Tuna's head changed into a fish, and the chopped-off tail became the conger eel that lives in the sea, and all the little pieces that Maui cut up so small, they changed into the fresh-water eels. We shall eat one of those tuna by the fire tonight.

Popo's eyes glistened as he thought of the tasty meal and the children laughed for they knew how their fat friend loved a well-cooked eel.

"You'll get fatter and fatter, Popo," Hine warned him.

"And as big as Tuna-roa," added Rata.

Popo laughed back at them and clipped Rata gently under the chin.

"I thought you were going to say as big as Tutunui the whale, you rascal. Then I would gobble you both up."

# HOW TAWHAKI CLIMBED UP TO THE SKYLAND

IN the stream that ran down the hill into the swamp there was a deep pool, overhung by a high bank. A pole had been set in this bank and from the top of the pole there hung many flax ropes. This was the moari of the village.

One morning all the children had gone down to the river. Some of them were swimming in the pool, but Rata and Hine were playing with the others on the moari. They grasped one of the rope-ends firmly, took it back to a little mound, and ran down the slope. At the edge of the bank they lifted their feet and swung right out over the pool. The rope made a circle through the air and brought them back to the mound again.

Presently one of the boys gave a shout as he swung out, and dropped feet first into the pool, slipping into the water like Kawau the cormorant.

The others soon followed him. Rata ran down the slope and swung over the pool, but he misjudged the distance and fell sideways into the water with a splash. When he came to the top everyone was laughing at him. Popo had come down to see the fun and he too was smiling.

"Were you any good at swinging, Popo?" asked Nene, who was one of the bigger boys.

Popo stood up straight. "I was the best in the whole tribe," he said proudly.

"Have a go at it now," Nene suggested, and everyone swarmed round Popo, shouting, "Come on, Popo. Show us how well you can do it."

Popo waved his hands and laughed, but Nene shouted, "Go on, Popo, or we'll never believe you."

Popo looked at the big boy closely and, turning on his heel, he took one of the flax strands and walked up the mound with it. He tested the rope, lumbered down the slope, and launched himself into the air. The moari pole bent with his weight and the rope went out in a big curve. As it began to come back there was a sharp crack, a great cry from Popo, and there was the fat old man tumbling head over heels into the pool. The water surged out and back again and Popo came up to the surface, puffing and blowing like a seal and laughing at the same time.

"There you are!" he cried as he scrambled ashore. "Who says I can't jump into the water now? But I've got no more wind left inside me. Some one will have to help me up the hill."

Rata and Hine ran up to their friend and helped him up the steep hill. Rata pulled and Hine pushed, and together they got him to the top. Popo sat and fanned himself with his hand.

"Let me sit down and get my breath," he said. "It's many years since I swung on the moari, and I never thought to do it again."

"Then why did you do it?" Hine asked, settling herself in the long grass by his side.

Pope scratched his head. "Nene said I was afraid," he replied.

"He didn't really mean it," Rata said quickly. "No one thinks that, Popo. You weren't afraid, were you?"

"Oh, yes, I was," Popo said. "That's why I did it. If I hadn't been afraid there wouldn't have been any need to do it."

Rata lay on his stomach watching the insects crawling through the grass and tried to think what the old man meant. Hine thought she knew, but anyway, here was a chance too good to miss.

"Tell us a story about a moari, Popo," she pleaded. Popo pulled out a long stalk of grass and chewed the end of it for a little while. Then he lay back and said, "Would you like to hear a story about a moari that stretched from the earth right up to the sky?"

"Please."

*Hine pulled and Rata pushed*

70

* * *

This is a story about Tawhaki who lived in the far-off days. Tawhaki's fame had spread afar, even up to the heavenly places. Looking down from her home in the sky, a daughter of the gods, who had heard of his mighty deeds, came down from the seventh heaven and lived with Tawhaki.

In time a daughter was born to them, and they all lived happily together until one day Tawhaki said something that hurt his wife. She caught her child up in her arms and rose up towards the sky. For a moment she rested by the carved figure on the roof gable.

"I shall never come back," she said to her husband, "but I know you will follow. My message to you is this: when you climb the heights of heaven, beware of the creeper that sways in the wind. Choose the one whose roots have gone deep into the earth. Farewell."

Tawhaki was very sad. He made up his mind to follow his wife, even to the heights of heaven. He knew he would never be happy again until he had found her.

Tawhaki visited his brother. "Come with me," he said.

"Where are we going?" asked Karihi.

"A long way, brother. I am going to look for my wife and daughter."

The brothers travelled together until they saw the creepers that stretched between earth and heaven. They hurried towards them, and there, holding them in her hand, sat their old, blind grandmother, Matakerepo. Ten taro roots were spread out in front of her. Tawhaki and Karihi came up quietly and watched the old lady. With her free hand she felt the roots and counted them slowly.

"One, two, three, four, five, six, seven, eight, nine—"

With a twinkle in his eye Tawhaki had quietly removed the tenth root. The old lady frowned. Thinking she had counted them wrongly, she began again.

"One, two, three, four, five, six, seven, eight—"

This time Karihi had taken a root. The old lady sat quite still. Then with a lightning move she snatched up a weapon and lashed out fiercely. Tawhaki and Karihi were watching her like hawks, and as the weapon sang through the air, they lay flat on their faces so that it passed over them.

Matakerepo put the weapon away and sat in silence. Tawhaki crept forward and struck her lightly on the face. The old woman was frightened. Letting go

71

of the creeper she had been holding, she cried pitifully, "Who is it? Who is there?"

Tawhaki struck her again across the eyes, and at once she could see. She looked into the faces of the men in front of her and gave a loud cry of welcome.

"It is you, Tawhaki, my grandson, and Karihi. Where are you going?"

"I am looking for my wife and child," Tawhaki said.

"Where are they?"

"They are above, somewhere in the Skyland."

"What made them go up into the sky, Tawhaki?"

"Hapai was a goddess, my grandmother. She came down to earth and lived with me for a while, but now she has gone back. I have come to look for them."

"There is your ladder to the skies," his grandmother replied, grasping the creepers again. "That is the way you must go. Beware the creepers that sway in the breeze; and when you are between heaven and earth, do not look down or you will get giddy. Look up!"

Karihi had been looking at the creepers. Without waiting to hear his grandmother's words he sprang up and clutched one that was drifting loosely above the earth.

As his fingers closed round the stem of the creeper, a gust of wind caught it, and swung him up into the sky. Forests, lakes and villages flashed past him and then disappeared as the giant swing swept him into the high-flying clouds. Karihi's breath caught in his throat as the swing dropped and he fell at lightning speed towards the earth. He tightened his grip as he swung almost to the ground. He felt that his arms would be dragged from his shoulders. As he raced by he could see Tawhaki and Matakerepo for an instant before he was carried far out over the sea and up into the clouds again. Then, as he swung back again, Tawhaki shouted, "Let go now." The creeper swept past and Karihi dropped off and fell at their feet.

"You have tried bravely," said Tawhaki kindly, "but our people need someone to look after them while I am away. Go back to the pa."

Tawhaki chose the firmly-rooted creeper and grasped the stem with his strong hands. He climbed steadily, holding on with his toes as well as his fingers. He kept looking up all the time. His grandmother's voice came to him fainter and fainter: "Hold fast, Tawhaki, hold fast. Let your hands hold fast."

*Tawhaki climbed steadily, looking up all the time*    page 72

Presently the voice faded away and there was no sound but the singing of the creeper in the wind. It was cold in that empty space, but he said the magic words that made him warm and strong.

At last the long, long climb was over. Tawhaki pulled himself up into the Skyland and stood among the trees and ferns. The trees grew close together, and there was no one in sight, but he could hear the thud of an axe and the sound of voices. He changed himself into the form of an old man, white of hair, thin and stooped, and pushed through the undergrowth.

He came to the edge of a clearing and stood watching. An unfinished canoe lay on the ground, and god-men were busy on it, cutting and smoothing the long hull.

They stopped their work to look at him. One of them shouted, "Look at the old man there. Come, it is nearly night. Let us finish now."

They threw down their axes and one of them said, "Come, slave, pick up the axes and follow us as quickly as you can."

Tawhaki picked up the tools and followed the god-men. As soon as they were out of sight, he turned and hurried back to the canoe. Throwing off his cloak, he began to smooth the sides. His skilled hands shaped the canoe carefully and well, and he worked hard for several hours.

Late that night he came to the village, old and bent under his load. He saw Hapai in the distance, and dropped his tools and walked over to her, but she did not know him in his disguise. He went to a sleeping-house and lay down on a mat, weary after his work.

The next morning Tawhaki was awakened by a cry: "Get up, slave, and take the tools to the canoe."

He straightened his back slowly and stood up. He picked up the axes and followed the god-men through the bush to the canoe. As they came into the clearing he heard their shout of surprise and smiled to himself. They walked round the half-finished canoe, looking at the

*. . . changed into an old man*

work that had been done since they left, and wondering what had happened.

When they were out of sight that night, Tawhaki went back, and adzed and planed till the canoe was nearly finished.

The next morning the canoe was the talk of everyone in the land of the gods. At nightfall Tawhaki returned and, taking off his disguise, carved the lovely bow and stern pieces. Tall and strong, he looked like a god himself, but as he worked, keen eyes were staring at him out of the undergrowth. This time the god-men had hidden in the bushes to see who had been working on their canoe.

When they saw Tawhaki they hurried to Hapai's house.

"Tell us," they said, "what does your husband look like? Is he big and handsome?"

"Yes."

"Tall and straight as a kauri tree?"

"Yes."

" Is his hair black and his eyes like stars?"

"Yes."

"Then it is Tawhaki who has finished our canoe!"

Presently an old man walked into the village and lowered the adzes from his back. He walked towards Hapai. She looked at him carefully. This man's back was bent. His face seemed wrinkled and old.

"Who are you?" she asked.

Tawhaki took no notice, but walked on until he came to his little girl.

He lifted her up and held her tightly in his arms. As he straightened himself, he grew young and handsome.

"It is Tawhaki!" the god-men cried, but Hapai lowered her head and cried with joy. Her husband had come to find her and she was happy again.

\* \* \*

Popo looked up. The sky had clouded over while he had been talking, and rain was sweeping across the inland hills. A flash of lightning lit the clouds, and a moment later a peal of thunder rolled among the hills.

"Listen," he cried, "you can hear the footsteps of Tawhaki in the Skyland!"

# HOW MAUI CAUGHT THE SUN

IN the early morning, as soon as the sun rose out of the sea, Rata and Hine went down to the foot of the cliffs and launched their tiny canoe in the still water. It was not really a canoe. Father called it a mokihi. It was made of dry flax stalks which were so light that when they floated in the water they hardly seemed to sink below the surface.

When the two children got in, it sank much deeper and the water got inside.

"It will never sink," Rata said. "The flax stalks are too light."

"But we had better keep close to the shore," Hine said.

"Of course. If anything happens, we can easily swim back to land. But nothing will happen. Come on, Hine."

They dipped their paddles into the water and the canoe swung slowly round and headed farther into the harbour.

They passed the rocks where the tiny waves gurgled and splashed, so close that they could see the crabs running about looking for food.

The sandy beaches were white as foam in the sunlight and already the cicadas were beginning their loud, creaking song which seemed to make the whole bush quiver.

At one place pohutukawa branches stretched so far out over the water that leaves brushed their faces as they paddled underneath. They played there for a while and then went on until they came to the farthest beach, where a big rock rose out of the water like an island when the tide was in. When they reached it the channel between the rock and the shore was wider than they had ever seen it before. It was twice the length of a man.

"This is our very own island for today," Hine said. They jumped on the rock and lifted the mokihi out of the water. There was a big hole, like the entrance to a cave, but you could crawl right through it. When you came to the other side, there were some shallow steps which seemed made for boys to climb up.

"I'm going up to the top, Hine."

Rata put his foot on the lowest step and pulled himself up. Then another step and another, until he could look down at his sister.

"Come on, Hine. It's easy." He caught hold of a little bush and climbed higher still, but the rock was crumbly and his feet slipped on the rotten rock.

Just in time he caught another bush, and for a moment he thought it would come right out, but it held him. A trickle of small stones rattled down the rock and fell on top of Hine, who had already climbed up three steps.

"Stay where you are," he shouted, "while I see whether we can get any farther."

The rock was still crumbly, but he found a ledge on which to put his toes. Then the rock sloped inwards and it was easier to hold on.

"It's all right, Hine. It's quite easy when you get past the steep bit. Hold on tight, and when you get to that bush, hold on to my hand and I'll pull you up."

Then they were standing side by side on the ledge and holding on to the rock. Little pieces came loose in their fingers, and already it seemed a long way down to their canoe.

"I don't think we had better go any farther," Hine said, but Rata laughed.

"Don't be scared," he said. "See, it's like climbing up a ladder. You go in front, and I'll hold your feet so they won't slip."

Hine was still scared, but she didn't like to say anything, because she didn't want Rata to think she was a silly girl. She held as tight as she could to the rocks, and scrambled up. It was easier than she thought, because Rata pushed. Once, when her foot began to slip, he caught her arm and held it.

It seemed a long time before they got to the top, but at last they were there. The flat part right at the top was larger than they thought, and there was a hump there, so they could sit down and rest their backs against it.

"This is fun, isn't it?" Rata said sleepily. "If we lie flat no one can see us.

Let's pretend that enemies are coming past. They won't think to look up. We can peep over the ledge and when they are gone, we can climb down and take our canoe back to the pa and warn Father that they are on their way."

Hine looked over the edge. On one side the rock was bare and smooth. The only way down was the way they had come up, and it was frightening to look at it. She shivered.

"You can't be cold!" Rata said.

Hine changed the subject. "Look, birds floating past without moving their wings! I would like to be a bird and float in the air without falling."

But to herself Hine thought how lovely it would be if she could open her wings and glide down without having to scramble down the rock.

Rata pulled some dried kumara out of the pouch which was tied round his waist and gave a piece to his sister. For a while they munched the food without speaking. The sun blazed down. They could see the light dancing on the rock where it was reflected in the water. It was very hot on top of the rock and everything was quiet.

*"Look, birds floating past without moving their wings"*

Presently the children were sound asleep. While they slept the tide went out. The sun began to sink slowly towards the hills. The water ebbed out of the channel that lay between the rock and the cliffs. It left a long, long stretch of mud flats where shellfish lay on the soft grey mud like flakes of sharp black rock, and tiny crabs scuttled busily from their holes.

At the top of the cliff there were some tall trees – puriri and totara and, a little farther inland, a giant kauri.

Had they been awake, the children might have thought of it as a huge net which had caught the sun in its meshes.

They stirred restlessly, for it was cold, now that the sun's rays had been cut off by the kauri tree. Rata rubbed his eyes and sat up. The sun was sending long rays of light through the branches of the kauri. The hills towards the harbour mouth still lay warm and bright in the sunshine, but under the cliff there was a deep blue shadow.

Rata stood up and looked round him. It was low tide now and between him and the shore there was a long stretch of mud. He went over to the edge and looked down. There was the canoe where they had left it, looking as small as a toy boat. He could not see where they had climbed up till he went right over to the other side. There were no bushes near the top. When he turned round and put his foot over the edge, feeling for somewhere to get a grip with his toes, the rotten rock crumbled and fell down the sides. The noise woke Hine. At first she could not make out where she was. All of a sudden she remembered.

She caught Rata by the arm.

*He could feel the loose flaky stones slipping*

"Be careful!" she said. "However are we going to get down?"

Rata laughed, but inside him he felt more like crying. The path that had seemed so easy going up looked impossible from above. He knew that the longer he waited the worse it would seem to be.

"It won't be so hard," he said, "but we will have to be careful. I will go first and you can follow me, Hine. If you slip I'll be there to hold you."

As he lowered his body over the edge he could feel the stones slipping and sliding. Whenever his toes felt a place to hold on to, the stones worked loose. He looked downwards over his shoulder, but everywhere the steep slope was smooth and bare. A large piece of rock gave way and he dropped suddenly, his hands clutching and scraping over the rough stones. His arms and legs and body were scratched as he tried frantically to hold on to something firm which would not come away in his hands.

He was sliding quickly now and his heart seemed to jump

inside him. And then, bump! His feet had been stopped by a ledge or rock. He felt cautiously about him. It was a ledge of solid rock, wide enough to stand on, that he remembered seeing as he came up, many hours before.

"It's all right, Hine," he said. "It's only the first part that's bad. Lower yourself over the edge and stretch your legs down. I'll be able to reach your feet, and then I can take your weight."

Hine did what Rata told her. It was frightening, but it made all the difference to know that her brother was there. She pressed tightly against the rocks and lowered herself till she was hanging at arm's length.

"Further, just a little bit further," Rata said.

"This is as far as I can go," she said, and then called out in a panic for her fingers were slipping.

"You're safe," Rata said, as he took the weight of her feet on his hands. "Hold yourself away from the rock and come down gently, while I hold you."

It was easy then, and soon the children were standing side by side.

"The worst is over now," Rata said. "It gets steeper further down but the rock is solid and doesn't give way. And there are even some bushes that we can hold on to."

Down they went, very carefully, Rata going first and putting up his hand to hold his sister if she slipped. But they both sighed with relief when they got to the bottom.

"I'll never go up there again," she said. "I suppose it isn't so bad, really. It's because you know how far you would fall if you did slip. But what are we going to do now? It will be dark soon and it's too far to carry the boat right to the water."

"Ah! You should have thought of that before," said a deep voice behind them. Both Rata and Hine jumped, and then laughed with relief.

"Oh, Popo, what a surprise you gave us! Where have you been?"

"On the beach round the point. I've got a good feed of pipis here," and he showed them a flax kit full of the shellfish. "The best pipis come from here," he said. "And now we must go home. You're far too late, you know. It will be dark and your mother will be worrying."

The old man tied the basket on his back, and took the children by the hand. We'll cut across the mud-flats to the far point, and that will save a lot of time."

They were silent for a while as they plodded over the flats, and the only sound was the squelching of their feet in the mud.

"Why are you so late?" Popo asked, after a while.

"Well, you see, we were on top of the rock," Hine replied, "and it was hot. There didn't seem anything to do and we fell asleep."

"And when we woke up," Rata continued, "the sun was low. It had been caught in the net of a kauri tree." And he told Popo what it looked like, covered with a web of branches.

"Just like in the long ago," Popo said. "Today went too fast for you, but once upon a time the sun really used to run across the sky and the days were so short that men could not do their work. Let me tell you about it, and it will make our journey seem shorter."

* * *

In the days when Maui lived with his brothers, everyone grumbled because the days were so short. Each morning the sun bounced out of the sea and travelled quickly across the sky. It was very awkward, but although everyone grumbled about it, no one did anything until Maui came. Only Maui watched the sun hurrying across the sky. Only Maui thought and thought until at last he knew what he had to do.

"Don't you think the days are too short?" he asked his brothers.

"Yes," they said. "They are not long enough for us to hunt, or fish, or work in our kumara gardens. That is why we have to play our games in the dark."

"Then we must make them longer."

They laughed at him. "You are always trying to do the impossible, Maui," they said. "Is the sun a bird, to be caught while it perches on a branch?"

"Yes," Maui replied. "I will catch it as if it were a bird sitting in a tree."

The brothers laughed louder still. "You must think you are a god, if you want to catch the sun."

Maui was growing angry. "You forget too quickly," he said. "You forget that it was Maui who tamed the fire you use. I am stronger than men, but I need your help. Tomorrow we will get up early and travel to where the sun rises. We will make a net of strong ropes and catch him, and tame him as if he were a bird."

He looked at them so fiercely that they were frightened.

"We would help you," they told him, "but it would be no use. The ropes would burn. The sun is so strong and fiery that the thickest ropes would burn, and we would be shrivelled up in the heat."

"Get your wives to bring flax and we will make the ropes now, before it gets too dark," Maui ordered. They called their wives and told them to bring the green flax leaves. Maui sat down with them and showed them how to plait them into strong ropes. Some were flat, others were round, and some were square, when they had finished. These were all the ways of plaiting flax which the Maori people still remember, though it was long, long ago when Maui first taught them how to make them. By the time night came they had a great pile of rope.

"Now we can sleep," Maui said, as the sun rushed from the sky and the twinkling stars came out all over the beautiful blue cloak of Rangi, the Sky Father. "We shall set out very early in the morning."

And so they did, long before the sun poked his head out of the sea, and the sky was still grey and cold. All that day they travelled, carrying long coils of the flax ropes. All the next day they kept on walking, and the next, until they reached the place of the sun where the sun rises. In the daytime they hid, but at night they came out and built a strong high wall of clay, right on the edge of the world. When the sun rose they would be able to shelter behind it from the heat. At the ends of the wall they built houses made of branches of trees. Above the place where the sun would rise they set a big rope noose and covered it with branches and green leaves so that it could not be seen.

When everything was ready they hid in the houses at the end of the wall, Maui in one and his brothers in the other. Presently the light grew stronger and stronger until they could hardly bear to look at it. A shaft of sunlight rushed across the wall. The brothers had one end of the flax rope in their hands.

"Steady," whispered Maui. "Wait till his head and paws are through the noose. A-ah! Now!"

The brothers pulled at the rope as hard as they could. Maui held the other end. The noose fell over the head of Tama the sun. Maui and his brothers felt him plunge and struggle like a fish caught by a hook.

"Hold tight," Maui called. They set their feet against the wall and tugged and tugged.

Tama, the sun, saw the wall, and the huts made of branches, and the ropes

*He struck the sun with a heavy club*

that stretched to the doors of the huts. He was angry and roared with pain. He caught the rope in his hands and tried to break it, but it was too strong for him.

He pushed with his feet against the earth, till the rope sang like insects in the bush in summer-time, and it began to slip through the fingers of the men who were holding it.

Maui tied the flax to the door of his hut and rushed out, bending low so that he was hidden by the wall. The fiery rays of the sun scorched his back and burnt his hair, but he rose up, shielding his face with his arm, and struck the sun with a heavy club. It was a magic weapon, made from one of the bones of his old grandmother.

Again and again he struck the sun god, until he stopped struggling and cried with pain. He fell on his knees and said, "Stop! Stop! Do you want to kill me?"

"No," Maui replied. "I am sorry I had to hurt you, Tama, but it was the only way to make you go more slowly. When you leap across the sky, the day goes so quickly that down on the earth there is not time for us to do all that we want. If I let you go now, will you promise to go more slowly, so that the days will be longer?"

"Yes," said Tama. "Your magic weapon has taken all my strength from me. I could not go quickly, even if I tried."

"Let go the ropes," Maui ordered his brothers. When they fell away, Tama stood up and began his journey across the sky. He went slowly, slowly, slowly, as he does to this very day.

* * *

"So that's how it was," Popo said. "Sometimes the day does seem to go quickly, but think what it was like before Maui tamed Tama, the Sun God!"

"Listening to stories makes the time go quickly, too," Hine said. "We are nearly home, and I thought it was going to be such a long walk. You are a lovely story-teller, Popo."

"Thank you, dear," the old man said with a twinkle in his eye which the children could not see, because it was so dark. "I enjoyed it, too !"

# HOW RATA MADE A GREAT CANOE

R ATA felt very sorry for himself. The other boys had gone over the hills and Hine was skipping with the girls, but he had a sore foot and could only hobble a few steps at a time. For a while he lay on the rocks watching the lizards sunning themselves, but he grew tired of being by himself. He began to feel miserable and lonely.

There was no one to talk to, so he limped along the forest track that led down to the water. His eyes brightened when he reached the sand, because the war canoes were drawn up on the beach.

He went up to the biggest canoe and climbed into it. He sat on the seat next to the tall stern-post and fingered the delicate wooden tracery that leapt up to the sky from the stern, wondering who had carved it, for this canoe had been made long before he was born.

He turned round and looked towards the bow which stretched its grinning figurehead out towards the open sea. He pretended that he was the steersman, and that the warriors were paddling the canoe out through the narrow passage between the rocks at the harbour entrance.

Armies are gathering by the far western sea.
Now dip your paddles! Pull! Speed the canoe!

went the song sung by the leader who stood amidships, keeping time for the men at the paddles. The canoes dipped and lifted to the ocean rollers as

Note: Here is part of the leader's song:
*Hui nga ope au ki te tai uru*
*Aue! Faia! Aue! Kaia hoki*

**84**

they headed into the open sea. The sunlight sparkled on the paddles and the wind whipped the spray into their faces.

The war canoe was beautifully balanced. She rolled a little as the men dug their paddles into the green and white water, but the headpiece lifted itself over the waves so that no water could curl above the splashboards. Under the seats the weapons were neatly stacked on the footboards. Rata could imagine the sun glinting on his father's greenstone club.

Still pretending that he was the steersman, he hung himself on the steering paddle and watched the canoe turning. Over his shoulder he could see the sentry on his platform at the edge of the pa keeping guard while the warriors were away. The water creamed behind in a quarter-circle. He watched the white streak fading into the water from which it had come. The other canoes crept out from shelter and turned into line behind him.

The wind had blown the hair into his eyes. It was getting colder, and the lashings against his shoulders had grown hard and uncomfortable. He turned on his side and heard the creak of the decking as the thin manuka stakes gave under him a little.

He shivered as he felt a cold wind on his skin, and opened his eyes. Everything was black. He looked up and saw the cold stars above him. Then he made out the lines of the canoe in the faint starlight, but the seats were empty.

He sat up, suddenly frightened. Waves were hissing up the beach, slapping against the bow like a bare hand. A queer light was dancing on the far rim of the canoe, and lighting up the sternpost. It came closer and Rata strained his ears. He could not hear footsteps, and he remembered all the stories he had heard about sea and land fairies, and how they sometimes stole children away.

Now the light was very close. It shone right into the canoe, lighting up everything so that Rata could see every knot and mark in the wood, and the cords that joined the splashboards to the hull. A blaze of light shone over everything, and he smelt the smoke of a wood torch.

"So there you are!" said a voice. "You *are* a brat. I've been looking everywhere for you. Have you been here all the time?"

"Oh, Popo!" Rata cried, "I am glad it's you. I must have fallen asleep."

Popo helped the boy out of the canoe and knocked the charred end off his torch. "How is your foot?"

Rata took a few paces to test it. "Much better now, Popo."

"Well, come on. It's time you were home."

Neither of them said anything as they climbed the hill, because Rata's foot was still hurting and Popo had no breath to spare. As they went along the narrow path that led into the pa, Popo asked the boy the question that had been puzzling him. "Why did you get into the canoe?"

Rata didn't say anything. The old man's fingers closed gently over his arm.

"Was it because you want to be a warrior and take your place on board some day, little one?"

Rata nodded. Popo couldn't see him, but he felt the movement and chuckled.

"I was just like that when I was your age," he said. "I used to dream about being a warrior.

I'm too fat now, and my fighting days are over, but there was a time . . ."

They were passing under the big carved figure that guarded the gate.

"Mind you," Popo went on, "a canoe is a good thing to love. Let it be well made and it becomes alive. It is a gift from the forest god, and it becomes a living thing of the sea god."

Popo guided the boy to the sleeping-house. "You are too tired to sit up tonight. Come and lie next to Popo and he will tell you about a man who had the same name as you, and how he built the *Great Joy*."

And this is the story that Popo told:

\* \* \*

*A gift from the forest to the sea*

This older Rata searched and searched the forest until he found the right tree for the canoe he was going to build. It was broad and straight, and so tall that it cast a long shadow on all the forest about it. Rata knew that this was the only tree good enough for his new canoe.

Thud! Thud! The keen edge of his greenstone adze bit into the hard wood with all his strength behind it. All afternoon he toiled, until with a great thump that shook the ground, the beautiful tree was down.

Proudly Rata lopped off its green head of leaves and branches.

"You will make a fine canoe, O tree," he said as he set off for home.

While he slept, strange things happened. The spirits of the forest were angry that the beautiful tree should have been cut down. They called the birds and insects together, and all the little people of the bush tugged at the great tree. It stirred uneasily on its grassy bed, and the air was filled with the sound of whirring wings; slowly the tree rose upright and stood in its own place. The tiny insects carried chips and grains of wood in their mouths and fitted them in place. As they worked, they sang this song:

> Fly together, chips and shavings,
> Stick fast together,
> Hold fast together,
> Stand upright again, O tree!

When Rata returned in the morning to begin the work of shaping the canoe, he rubbed his eyes. For a moment he thought he had made a mistake, but when he looked round him he could see broken twigs and leaves, and the groove where the trunk of the tree had pressed into the ground; but there it stood, where it had been growing for many times the life-span of a man.

Rata sang a song of magic to protect himself against the spirits before taking up his adze and cutting the tree down again. He worked quickly, and soon it lay with its head cut off.

*The spirits of the forest were angry*

87

He ran his adze along the straight trunk, taking off the curling shavings. By nightfall the graceful lines of the canoe had been shaped out of the timber, and only the hollowing of the hull remained to be done. But when he came back next morning, not a sign of his work was left. Through the night the birds and insects had raised the tree, until it stood proudly lifting its waving branches above the lesser trees of the forest.

For the third time Rata chopped it down. Without troubling to work at it any more, he picked up his adze and walked towards the village. When he was out of sight of the tree, he turned from the track and slipped noiselessly through the ferns until he could see the place where it was resting. As it began to grow dark, he heard the song of the birds and insects:

> *Fly together, chips and shavings,*
> *Stick fast together,*
> *Hold fast together,*
> *Stand upright again, O tree!*

He could see the flash of wings. Never had there been so many forest birds together at one time. Weka and Kiwi ran round the fallen tree; Fantail fluttered anxiously above it; Ruru and Kaka and Kakapo and thousands of others were pulling and tugging at it. He looked closer and saw insects running to and fro, falling over one another in their eagerness to help.

Rata felt the force of the magic song. His own feet seemed to leave the ground. Then the tree rose upwards, almost hidden by the fluttering wings of the birds. It stood up straight with the sharpened point of the trunk, where the adze had bitten into it, resting lightly on the point of the stump. Insects swarmed upwards from the ground, fitting the tiniest splinters into place.

"Ha!" cried Rata, springing up and rushing towards the tree, "It is you who have spoiled my work!"

The birds crowded round him. "Was it you, Rata, who dared to kill the heart of this tree?"

Then Rata felt ashamed. "What shall I do?" he asked. "I wanted a canoe to travel far over the sea on a sacred journey. My father died in a distant land and I want to bring his body back to our homeland. That is why I cut down this totara tree."

*The birds of the forest crowded round Rata*    page 88

All the birds and insects cried, "Go back to your place, Rata. We will make your canoe."

Rata turned away and left the building of the mighty canoe to the tiny forest people. In a day it was made – *Riwaru*, the *Great Joy*.

It was dragged through the forest on sapling skids and launched on the sea. Proud and stately it rode, and within its strong bulwarks there was room for a hundred and forty men. They took their places, the fighting men of Rata, and plied their paddles until *Riwaru* skimmed the waves like a gull as it flies above the water, lifting to the incoming waves.

\* \* \*

Little Rata's head was nodding. Popo stopped and pulled a mat over the boy. Then he lay down himself. Rata smiled in his sleep, and Popo wondered whether he was dreaming about the other Rata and the *Great Joy*.

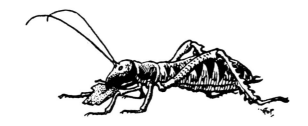

# HOW KAE STOLE THE WHALE

"LET'S play darts," said one of the bigger boys after the evening meal. With whoops of delight, Rata and his friends scrambled down through the forest that clothed the harbour slopes and came out by the raupo swamp. Each boy chose a straight reed and hurried with it to the beach where the canoes were kept.

Two of them built a mound of wet sand to the height of their knees, smoothing it over carefully. One of the bigger boys picked up his reed dart and spat on it, saying some words over it. He threw it so that it struck the heap, glanced off again and stuck point first into the white sand.

When Rata toed up to the mark the beach was littered with darts, some lying flat, and others with their points buried in the sand. As Rata's dart struck the little sandhill, a puff of wind caught it and blew it sideways to the water's edge. He was not a good dart-thrower yet. Some of the boys could throw their darts far down the beach.

A surprise came as it was getting dark. Big Nene had whispered to his reed for a long time before he drew it back. With a smooth under-arm swing, he tossed it towards the sandhill. As it struck the mound, it seemed to glide like a bird. In the growing dusk it flew down the beach and slithered almost out of sight. Then it was too dark to play any more.

"How did you manage to throw your dart so far, Nene?" asked Rata as he climbed the hill with the winner.

"Because I'm very strong," replied Nene with a laugh.

"Yes, I know," Rata said seriously, "but it wasn't that altogether, was it?"

90

He really wanted to know. "You didn't do nearly so well until your last throw."

Nene looked down at Rata, who was just a dark shape under the tree. He looked round and listened, but no one else was near. He lowered his voice. "I learned a new charm from the priest last night," he said softly. "Come into the forest with me tomorrow morning and I will teach it to you, little one," he said.

Rata's eyes were shining as he came out on to the marae, the open space in the middle of the houses. He knew he was growing up, because Nene was going to share a secret with him. Hine was walking towards the big house and Rata caught up with her. It was lighter up here because there were no trees to screen the glow of the evening sky, but the shadows of the hills were black on the water. A cold breeze was blowing in from the sea, and the big house seemed hot when they got inside. Most of the people were already sitting down.

Flames were leaping from the fire pits sunk in the floor. The paua-shell eyes of the carved figures on the posts that held up the ridgepole winked like stars on a frosty night.

Brother and sister crept over to the low side wall and sat down with their backs to the laced reed panels. They could see everything that went on, but at the far end of the house the smoke drifted about like mist.

Presently Popo lumbered across and sat between them. They made room for him on the floor mat.

"Will you dance tonight, Popo?" asked Hine with a twinkle in her eye.

"Not tonight," said Popo solemnly. "When I was young I was the best dancer in the tribe. Now I get too hot."

"Poor Popo," said

*"I learned a new charm from the priest last night"*

91

Hine. "But you can still watch, can't you? See, there is our grandmother."

Everyone was looking at old Muri, who had thrown down her outer cloak and stood in the open space in the middle. She was tall and thin, with short grey hair and wrinkled face. A bunch of soft, white albatross-down hung from her ear, while the lovely greenstone tiki that Hine hoped would be hers some day hung from a cord round her neck.

Muri clapped her hands on her thighs and the flax skirt she wore made a dry rustling sound. Then the old lady began to dance.

"See, it is beautiful," Hina whispered. "She is like the son of the Summer Girl."

"And who was the son of the Summer Girl?" Popo asked, because he wanted to find out how much his little friend had remembered of his teaching.

"His name was Tane-rore," Hine replied. "The Summer Girl was his mother, and his father was the Sun. We can see him in the summer time when the air dances in the heat, because that is the Dancing of Tane-rore. And that is what Muri's dance reminds me of," she finished dreamily.

The old woman had sunk on to the floor exhausted. Popo stroked Hine's arm and looked at the little girl approvingly. "You have a good memory, little Hine," he said. "Now look at the young women of the tribe."

They had come out from the shadows and were sitting in line. The pois at the end of their long strings danced in time with the song. The girls swayed backwards and forwards, and the watchers could almost hear the splash of the paddles as they sang their canoe song.

"It is the song of Hine-te-iwaiwa," Popo said.

"Who was Hine-te-iwaiwa?" Rata asked promptly.

The old man settled himself more comfortably on the mat, and Hine cuddled close to him.

\* \* \*

It all began with Tinirau and his pet whale, he said. You see, Tinirau was a chief who had just become the father of a baby boy. No one was good enough to baptise the baby, Tinirau thought, except Kae, the famous priest who lived far away on the mainland. Canoes were sent from Tinirau's home on the Magic Island, and they brought Kae back with them.

92

When the baby had been baptised, Tinirau and Kae walked together on the beach. They reached the rocks at the end, and Tinirau stopped and shouted "Tutunui!" in a loud voice. Kae looked round in surprise, because he could not see anyone there.

Presently something like a huge rock rose out of the sea. It was a whale. The water rushed off its back like a waterfall and two spouts of vapour soared in the air and drifted away on the breeze. Kae had never seen a whale so close before. It came closer until its body was touching the rock on which the two men stood.

Tinirau cut a piece of flesh from the side of the monster. The whale rolled its tiny eyes at him, gave a sigh, and slid back into deep water. Tinirau was laughing at Kae, whose eyes were still very big. "Have you never seen my pet whale?" he asked. "That is Tutunui. He is a great friend of mine. He takes me over the sea faster than any canoe."

Kae scarcely knew what to say.

"But what did you cut the flesh for?"

"You will see when we take it from the cooking oven, and you can sink your teeth into it."

That night Kae tossed uneasily on his mat in the Strangers' House. He had eaten too much whale-meat and he could not sleep. As he lay awake he longed to have Tinirau's whale for himself.

When the time came for Kae to go back to his own village, Tinirau had a canoe waiting for him.

"Tinirau," said Kae, "are you satisfied with the way I baptised your son?"

"Yes," Tinirau replied.

"Do you feel that it will make him a great fighter?"

"I am sure of that, too."

"But perhaps the priest of your own tribe could have done just as well?"

"No, no," Tinirau said quickly, because he did not want to make Kae angry. "No one is so wise or clever as you, Kae."

"Then I have a favour to ask."

"Speak."

"It is this. Call Tutunui and make him carry me back to my place."

"But you would be much more comfortable in the canoe," Tinirau said.

Kae frowned, and Tinirau spoke quickly. He knew it was not wise to

*The strange voyage began*

make Kae angry. "I was only joking. He shall take you to your home. Only remember this, Kae. When you get near the shore, Tutunui will shake himself. When he does that, jump off quickly and swim ashore."

"I know," Kae said impatiently.

Tinirau went down to the beach and lifted his hands to his mouth.

"Tutunui!" he shouted, and in a few minutes they saw the whale coming close to the shore.

Kae scrambled on to his back and his strange voyage began. It did not take long, and soon they came close to the shore. The whale shook himself to show Kae that it was time for him to jump off, but Kae took no notice. Tutunui shook himself again, but Kae pressed heavily on his back, repeating spells until the whale sank in the shallow water. Tiny grains of sand filled his blowholes, and with a last shudder, Tutunui lay still and died.

There was great fun in Kae's pa that night. Everyone had plenty of tasty whale flesh to eat.

Far away on the Magic Island Tinirau looked in vain for his whale to come back. He lifted his head and smelt the land breeze. From the mainland there came the delicious smell of cooked food, and Tinirau knew what had happened. The chief called his people together at once. "Kae has stolen my whale. Who will go with me to punish him?"

The warriors leaped eagerly to their feet. "We will go with you, Tinirau!" they shouted.

"No," said a soft voice. "I will go. I, Hine-te-iwaiwa."

The people looked at her in astonishment. "Yes, I will go, and other women of our tribe. Kae has many fighting men. Let the women go. We will bring him back to you without shedding of blood, O Tinirau."

A little time went by, until there came a night when people were laughing in Kae's house. Hine-te-iwaiwa and many other women of Tinirau's tribe were there. They had travelled from village to village, entertaining people with their songs and dances. No one knew who they were. Now the men and women of Kae's tribe had come to see them.

As they danced, Hine and her friends looked sharply about them. Somewhere in this house was their enemy Kae. They would know him when he laughed, for his teeth were broken and uneven.

Everyone laughed at their jokes and merry dances. Only one man sat without a smile on his face. But the women had saved their best item till the last, and even the silent man was forced to laugh. When he put back his head and opened his mouth, the girls could see his ugly broken teeth. It was Kae!

When the fire had died down and all was quiet in the house, the women sang a soft song of magic which made everyone sleep soundly. They lifted Kae gently, wrapping his sleeping-mat round him, and carried him to their canoe. Kae slept his enchanted sleep as they paddled back to Motu-tapu, the Magic Island. The dawn had just brightened the sky as they lifted him from the canoe and carried him to Tinirau's house.

It was broad daylight when Kae woke up. He was sleepy and thought he was still in his own house. Tinirau opened the door and cried, "Greetings, Kae."

"Why have you come to my house?" asked Kae.

"Oh, Kae," Tinirau said, "Why have you come to my house?"

"What do you mean? This is my house."

"Look round you, Kae."

Kae looked round. The house seemed different. The reed pattern on the walls was different. The carved posts were different. He looked out of the door, past Tinirau, and saw only the grinning faces of strangers. And then he knew that he was in the home of his enemies.

* * *

Popo sat up. The poi dancers had gone back to the shadows. Hine looked up into Popo's face.

"But what happened to Kae?" she asked.

"He learned that people who steal whales get punished," he said with a grin, and sent both the children off to bed.

96

*Kahukura and the magic fishermen*    page 101

# HOW KAHUKURA FOUND THE MAGIC NET

"LET'S follow Popo," Rata said to his sister one afternoon. Their old friend had disappeared into the forest. They had waited to see him come out on to the beach, but he did not appear.

"Look, there he is," Hine said suddenly. Popo had gone right through the broad tongue of forest that spread across the hillside, and now they could see his head showing above the flax bushes in the distance.

The children ran through the forest in the cool shade of the trees and came out on the sun-baked bank that looked over the inner harbour. Presently they saw Popo bending over something in the distance. They crept up behind him and looked through the grass. He was half hidden in a flax bush.

Hine was going to call to him, but Rata whispered, "Wait! See what he is doing."

Popo pushed his way into the flax leaves until he was in the heart of the bush. He lifted a tender young leaf and held it above his head.

"Oh!" cried Rata excitedly, "He's going to make a new net. That's the men's leaf. Listen carefully."

Popo was singing. It was a funny old song about nets being full and fish plenty, but they could not understand many of the words. He stopped, and the children listened. Far away one of the village dogs barked as if it had seen a kiwi. Close beside them the stream sang its tinkling song, and a little farther off there was a shrill humming from the sun-drenched insects, but it was quiet on the hillside. In the silence they heard a long squeaking sound from the flax bush.

"The net will be lucky. The women's flax blade squeaked as it came out,"

Hine said excitedly, but she spoke too loud and Popo looked round.

"Ah, you rascals," he cried. "Popo's eyes are too sharp for you. You've no right to be here when I'm making a net, you know."

"We're sorry, Popo," Rata said, "but it doesn't matter much if it's only going to be a little net, does it?"

"Not very much. Little net, little magic. Big net, big magic. Remember that, my little birds. But now Popo is old, and perhaps he will pass on to you a tiny bit of magic."

He held up the two flax leaves. "Look closely at the broken ends. See, they are all ragged. That shows that it will be a good net, a lucky one, because the spirits of the fish that will be caught some day have already nibbled the ends."

He sat down on a tussock and the children watched his fingers looping and threading the flax cords until, as the sun was low in the sky, the little hand net began to take its proper shape.

"It grows late," Popo said. "I will finish it tomorrow."

"We'll come and watch you again, Popo. When I'm a man –" Rata broke out and jumped to his feet. "Look," he cried, "the men are bringing in the big net!"

Down on the water a great half moon lay across the bay. It was the thousand-foot net of the tribe. They watched for a few moments and saw that it was slowly growing smaller.

"Come on," Rata shouted, and the children plunged down the hillside holding Popo's hands.

He panted and sobbed and called on them to stop, but it was no use. Popo was like a sledge made from the head of a ti-palm when it dashes down a slope, and nothing except the flat beach at the bottom could stop him. They landed in a laughing heap on the sand.

When they had climbed over the rocks on the point, the canoes were

*Spirits of the fish*
*nibbled the flax*

98

already ashore, and they could see the wooden floats of the net bobbing up and down on the waves. The men were pulling it ashore, and they could hear the rustle of the stone sinkers as they were dragged over the sand and the splashes of the fish as they leaped into the air and fell back again.

Soon a darting silvery mass filled the shallow water enclosed by the net, and everyone watched in silence while the priest picked up a fish and held it close to his mouth. He whispered to it and then tossed it into the water beyond the net.

"Little fish, go and tell your brothers to come to our great net," Popo whispered under his breath.

It was a wonderful catch, and Popo was proud of the tribal net which he had helped to make.

"It is a very good thing to live in the northland," Popo said to the children, "because it was here, at the tail of Maui's fish, that Kahukura found the first net."

"Who was Kahukura?" Hine asked.

* * *

Kahukura was a chief. He was not like other men, because his skin was pale and his hair was coloured like the sun. The old men of the tribe used to sit in the sun by the house wall and watch him as he stood looking out over the Ocean of Kiwa. When he did that, his spirit used to wander in this land of the far north, among the sand dunes where the gulls wheel and cry and the spirits of the dead march on to the giant pohutukawa tree that overhangs the Doorway of Death.

Time after time a dream had come to Kahukura, a dream of something waiting for him in the distant northland. The chief sighed and turned his back on the sea. As he walked back to the pa he could see the young men looking over their fishing lines and mending the bone hooks. In Kahukura's coastal pa there were many mouths to

*He whispered to the fish*

99

*Sometimes rain chilled him*

feed, and the canoes went out in all weathers with trailing lines so that the people might have a tasty morsel of fish to eat with their fernroot and kumara and birds and rats.

That night, as Kahukura lay on his mat, a ghostly voice kept saying to him: "Go north, Kahukura. Go alone. Go to Rangiaowhia, to Rangiaowhia, to Rangiaowhia."

While his people were asleep, Kahukura rose softly and crept out of the house. Day after day he travelled north. He stopped only when weariness overcame him. He took his rest in the shelter of rocks and on mossy patches in the forest, and in the tall grasses. Sometimes the rain chilled him, and sometimes he walked under the hot sun as it moved slowly across the sky. Sometimes Marama, the Moon, looked down and smiled at the tiny figure that walked on so steadily towards the end of the land.

One night as Kahukura stood on the sands of a northern beach he heard the sound of music which came stealing across the ocean. He looked across the water and in the darkness twinkling lights appeared. The music grew louder and he heard the sound of paddles, and of voices laughing and singing. Canoes were gliding over the water and everywhere there were little dancing lights. Kahukura knew that this was Rangiaowhia, the fishing ground of the fairy people.

He crept down to the water's edge. The darkness hid him from the eyes of the fairy fishermen. They were much closer to the shore now, and he heard them crying, "The net here!

**100**

The net here!" He could not understand the words. What was the "net"? The only ways that Kahukura knew of catching fish were by hook and line and spear. These were fairy words and this must be fairy magic!

The canoes touched the shore and the fairies jumped out. Kahukura could see a strange bubbling line out in the water. Inside the line the fish were jumping up in hundreds, and he could hear the slap-slap of their bodies as they fell back again. The bubbling line must be the net! It was a magic way of fishing that caught hundreds of fish together instead of one at a time on a hook or a spear.

The fairies were pulling the ends of the net. Kahukura came closer and mixed with them. His skin was fair like theirs and in the darkness they did not notice that they were being helped by a mortal. He pulled at the flax rope and felt wet knotted rushes passing through his hands.

*Kahukura listened to the music*

The net came up on to the beach in a last rush. The fairies picked up the fish and strung them on cords, each working by himself in haste lest the dawn should come before they were finished. Kahukura strung fish on cords with the others, but he did not tie a knot at the end, so that when he lifted his string, the fish fell off on to the sand. One of the fairies saw them falling and came to help Kahukura to tie the knot properly. When he had gone Kahukura untied it again. Then he lifted the string and again the fish fell off. Another fairy came to help him.

Time and again the chief played this trick on the fairies. He was watching the eastern sky. Over the sea there was now a faint tinge of light. It grew stronger and stronger. The fairies were running to the canoes with their strings of fish, but still Kahu's fish dropped off his unknotted cord, and still the fairies helped him.

A bright beam of light shone over the ocean, lighting up the clouds. A cry of dismay came from the fairies. At last they had seen that a man was with them. They rushed down the beach to their canoes, but they were too late. The sand had turned to gold in the sunlight and the fairies scattered and disappeared. The canoes shrank and crumbled until nothing was left but a few bundles of rushes and flax leaves. The fairy voices died away.

Kahukura stood alone on the shining beach. The fish were gone. Only one thing had been left behind and Kahu held it in his hands. It was the thing that the fairies had called a net – a pile of flax cords tied in a strange pattern and wet with sea water.

* * *

"That was the father of all nets," Popo said. "You see, Kahukura took it home with him, and as he went he studied the knots and found out how they were tied. There is always big magic in a net because the fairies taught us how to make them."

"It was a good story," said Hine sleepily in the darkness.

"It is a true story, child," Popo replied. "You saw the big net tonight and the food it caught. Remember every time the net goes out, that it is the secret which Kahukura won from the fairy fishermen at Rangiaowhia in the long ago."

# HOW KUMARAS CAME TO MAORILAND

FOOD had been scarce in the village for a long time, but a few days ago the first kumara crop had been lifted, and everyone was looking forward to a big feast.

Rata and Hine and their friend Popo had been sitting in the sunshine with their backs to the heap of logs beside the wet-weather cooking-shed. They were watching the women getting the big meal ready. Piles of firewood had been gathered and placed on top of light brushwood in the earth pits. Smooth stones had been placed on top of the wood, and then the fires were lit. The flames had leaped and crackled and the air had danced in the hot sunshine. "Remember Tane-rore?" Popo had said. Presently the wood had burnt away and the clean, hot stones lay at the bottom of the pits.

The women had spread a layer of green leaves and twigs on the stones, and the food was laid on top. More leaves were scattered over the food, and water was sprinkled on until steam began to rise from the pits. Flax mats were laid in layers, and the pit was filled with earth which was stamped hard.

After that there was nothing to do except look at the women plaiting little food baskets from the broad flax leaves, but the three watchers kept their eyes fixed on the place where the food was cooking under the ground.

Time had passed slowly, but at last the sun touched the western hills. People came from every direction as if by magic as the earth was dug out and gushes of steam came out of the pits. The mats were lifted, the leaves were tossed aside, and the kumaras, fish and birds were lifted out and placed in the baskets. A delicious smell filled the air, and in a very little while tongues were stilled as the food was eaten.

Rata and Hine had taken a basket over to Popo, who was too comfortable to move, and they ate in silence, blowing their fingers as they lifted up the hot kumaras.

"Lovely!" said Popo as he came to the bottom of the basket. "It's worth being hungry for a long time to have such a meal as this," and he rubbed his stomach and sighed contentedly. He had had an enormous feed, and the children had eaten nearly as much.

"Wouldn't it be awful if there were no kumaras," Hine said, licking her fingers.

"Terrible," Rata agreed. "Did they always grow in our land, Popo?"

The old man settled himself more comfortably and thought for a while. "No," he said at last. "Kumaras came to us from far across the sea on the back of a great bird. Would you like to hear the story, children?"

"Yes, please," they said together.

\* \* \*

This story is about Pou the Strong. He was a great chief, and he had a little boy whom he loved dearly. Anything that the baby's hands reached for, Pou was ready to get for him. As the boy grew older, Pou noticed that he was always putting out his tongue, and always in the same direction. When he was lying down, he would roll over to poke out his tongue, and when he was standing he would turn round so that it would point the same way. Pou talked it over with his wife, and they decided that the little boy was hungry, and that he was pointing to where he knew there was good food.

*Over the endless plains of the ocean he sailed*

104

"Then I will find it for him," said Pou the Strong. He took his weapons and some food and pushed his canoe into the sea. His wife watched him as he paddled away. The canoe became a tiny speck in the ocean, and then it was gone.

Over the endless plains of the ocean he sailed, day after day, until at last the canoe came to the beach of a distant country. Pou jumped ashore to meet the people who had seen him coming and were waiting for him.

He soon made friends with them, and they shared their evening meal with him. Pou cried out with delight as he tasted the steaming vegetables. They were sweeter than any fernroot he had ever tasted, for they were kumaras. Pou had never heard of them. They did not grow in our long bright land in those days, and he knew at once that this was the very food that his son had been asking for.

He stayed in the new country for a while, but all the time he longed to be back in his own home, watching his son as he ate the lovely food. But alas! His canoe had gone. Perhaps a storm had battered it to pieces on the shore; perhaps the tide had gently lifted it till it floated away.

The great chief Tane was his friend, and one night, as they lay side by side on their sleeping mats, Pou told his troubles to Tane.

Tane raised himself on his elbow. "There is only one way," he said. "It is a dangerous way, but a man who seeks his home after long journeying thinks little of danger."

"I have faced dangers as I sailed the Ocean of Kiwa," Pou said. "There is no greater danger anywhere than in the sea, when there is only a hollow log between a man and the endless waters."

"You were in danger then," Tane agreed, "and you will be in danger as you return. You must travel on the back of the Great Bird of Ruakapanga."

"The Great Bird of Ruakapanga!" Pou whispered. "But how will he take me?"

*Tasting the kumara*

"If you climb on his back and hold closely to him, he will fly with you to your home. Halfway there, on a great island, lives Tama the Ogre. You must beware of him, for if you fall into his clutches, he will kill you!"

"How can I escape him, Tane?"

"You must wait until the sun is setting. Just before it sinks into the ocean, it blinds the ogre, and if you are bold, you can fly past him before he can catch you."

Early next morning Pou took two baskets of kumaras to use as seeds, and climbed on to the back of the huge bird. It beat its great wings and lifted Pou and his heavy load as if they had been light as feathers. As it headed southwards, Pou looked down and saw the tiny figures of his friends far below. Tane was there too, shading his eyes, as he watched Pou begin his flight.

After a long time the bird flew close to the perilous island. Pou tugged at its neck and it flew more slowly until the lower edge of the sun touched the sea. Then in a blaze of light they flew past the hill.

There was a roar when Tama heard the beating of the giant wings, but before he could see where they were, they had passed and the danger was over.

*. . . lifted Pou and his heavy load as if they had been feathers*

*There was a roar when Tama heard the beating of the giant wings*

* * *

"Did he really get home safely?" asked Hine.

"Of course he did," Rata said scornfully. "And the little boy had as much kumara to eat as he wanted. We shouldn't have had kumara to eat tonight if he hadn't reached home again, should we, Popo?"

The old man looked at Rata with a smile. "Yes, Pou got home safely, and his son never cried for food again. But even if the chief hadn't got back, I still think we'd be eating kumara tonight, Rata."

"Why, where would it have come from?"

"Well, you see, there were seed kumaras in the Canoes of the Great Fleet*," Popo said with a big grin, and Rata nodded because, like every Maori boy, he knew that the Fleet had brought the Maori people themselves to their own land of Aotearoa.

*The Great Fleet was the succession of canoes that brought Maori to Aotearoa.

# THE STORY OF HATUPATU & THE OGRESS OF THE BIRDS

THERE was great excitement in the pa. While everyone was sitting down for the morning meal, with the fish and kumaras steaming in the flax baskets, there was a loud cry from the sentry on the watch-tower.

"Canoes! Three war canoes!"

The food was forgotten as everyone rushed to the palisades and looked at the sea. The sun was shining brightly, but there was a fresh north-west wind. Three canoes were coming towards them, sometimes half hidden in spray as the waves crashed against their bows, and sometimes hanging in full view as they were lifted high out of the water. As they watched, the canoes grew bigger and bigger.

"They are heading this way," said Ruru, the father of Hine and Rata. "We cannot tell whether they are friends or enemies, so we must be ready for them. Let the women and children fill the calabashes with water. The boys can put stones on the watch-towers, ready for throwing at the warriors if they attack the pa. Let the men bring their weapons and come with me to the outer stockade."

Everyone hurried off. Hine and Rata helped the women to fill the calabashes.

"Why are we doing this?" Hine said to Rata.

"In case they throw fire on to the roofs of the whares," Rata said. "Then we will put the fire out with the water. Oh, I wish I was big so that I could be a warrior and fight with Father."

He looked down at the palisades. The warriors had closed the great gate, which was the only way into the pa. The men looked between the big, strong posts and fingered their weapons.

Ruru had climbed up on to the watch-tower. "The canoes have entered the harbour," he shouted, and they all stopped what they were doing to listen to him.

"Rata, I think I'm frightened," Hine said. "What will happen to us if they were to break into the pa?"

"They'll never get in while Father is here," Rata said scornfully. "He is a great warrior. But listen."

Ruru's voice rang out again. "The canoes have been pulled up on to the sand, and the warriors are coming up the track from the beach. They are armed, but there are women behind them, so they may be coming in peace. But that may only be a trick. The women and young people must shelter behind the whares."

He waited till they had hidden themselves, and then climbed quickly down the ladder and hurried to the stockade.

By now they could all see that the strangers were climbing the path, but they were still too far away to be recognised. Silence had fallen on the pa, and everyone waited without speaking. Now the visitors were out of sight in a dip in the ground, but when they came into sight again everyone would know whether it was to be peace or war.

"It is Temuera!"

"Ah!" Popo's great voice rang out. "It is Temuera!"

At once there was a buzz of voices and the women came out from behind the whares.

"Who is it?" Hine asked her mother.

Mother smiled as she put her arm round her daughter. "Temuera is a very old friend of ours," she said. "Your father and he fought together against the people of Taranaki when they were young, and they are like brothers. There will be a great feast tonight, for Temuera's ancestors came to this land in the same canoe as our ancestors many, many years ago. Let us go down and see what is happening."

Temuera's warriors were drawn up in rows

on the piece of ground beyond the big ditch in front of the pa. Ruru's men had opened the gate and had put down the logs which made a bridge across the ditch.

They ran swiftly across and spread out in two lines facing their visitors and, at a signal from Ruru, squatted down. Temuera stood in front of his men and raised his greenstone mere. It quivered in his hand, and every man raised his right foot and then his left foot. As if they were one man, they jumped high in the air and began a fierce war dance until the ground seemed to shake. As they danced and sang, and made terrible faces, they kept time by slapping their hands against their thighs. At last the dance came to an end with a tremendous shout. Waving their weapons, they rushed up to Ruru and his men, who stood still. The visitors stopped just short of them and retreated. Then it was the turn of Ruru and his warriors. They jumped higher, they shouted louder, they rushed more fiercely at their visitors.

The mock war was over. Hine and Rata were not frightened for they had seen it happen before. Ruru and Temuera put their arms round each other and pressed their noses together while the tears ran down their cheeks. The women came together and everyone laughed and talked as they entered the pa.

"You must help," Mother said. "There is so much to be done. The fires must be lit, the kumaras and the fish cooked, the preserved pigeons brought out of the storehouses, and fresh puwha gathered. This is a wonderful time for us, because Temuera and his people have come a long, long way to visit us."

When the stars came out that night, the visitors had eaten so much food that they could hardly move, and Ruru's people felt the same. It had been a wonderful feast.

But the excitement was not over. The young men and women were soon feeling lively. Ruru stood up and welcomed Temuera; then Temuera said how glad he was to be with his friends. And then the dances! The girls gave the loveliest poi dances and the young men showed how well they could dance the haka.

It grew very hot in the big meeting-house. Hine and Rata could hardly keep their eyes open. They were too tired for stories, but Popo said, "Tomorrow morning, children! You must go to sleep now, but tomorrow morning I will get my old friend Rangi to tell you a story you have never heard before."

And this was the story that Rangi told to Hine and Rata and all the other children in the pa the next morning, as they sat beside the palisades in the shadow of the big pohutukawa tree.

* * *

In our part of the country the fire gods walk with us, Rangi said. Boiling pools of water lie outside the doors of our whares, where we cook our food. Hot mud bubbles up from the earth and great geysers send boiling water high into the air. You must try to imagine this strange country as I tell you the story of Hatupatu and his brothers.

Hatupatu was the youngest boy in the family. His brothers were famous hunters. When they went far away into the forests on their bird-catching

*They left the scraps for Hatupatu*

expeditions, they always took Hatupatu with them. Poor Hatupatu had to stay in the tiny whare they had built, and do all the work. When his brothers came home at night, Hatupatu cooked the evening meal. The elder brothers took the best birds and left the scraps for Hatupatu. When he complained they laughed at him.

"You are only a slave," they said. "You will never be a hunter. Stay at home like a woman, and do as you are told."

Sitting by the fire, red-eyed with the smoke, Hatupatu felt sorry for himself.

One night he decided that if his brothers would not feed him properly, he would look after himself.

The next day he waited until his brothers had gone. Then he hurried to the storehouse. His mouth watered as he looked at the rows and rows of baskets, filled with fat tasty birds. Carefully he chose two of the fattest, tenderest pigeons and cooked them in his earth oven with fern root and kumaras. When the food was

*The Birdwoman carried Hatupatu away*    page 115

ready he ate and ate till he could not cram another piece into his mouth.

All that afternoon he basked happily in the sunshine, but as the sun got low in the sky he began to think of his brothers and he was afraid. "They will beat me when they know I have taken their food," he thought. "Perhaps I can make them think that an enemy has been here."

He went back to the storehouse and knocked over some of the baskets. Then he jabbed a spear into himself in a number of places, trying not to hurt himself too much. Soon he was covered with blood, and he lay down on the path outside.

When his brothers returned they picked him up and carried him inside.

"What has happened?" they asked.

"A war-party came and broke into the storehouse," Hatupatu said in a weak voice. "I tried to keep them off but they attacked me with spears. Then I did not remember any more until you came back and carried me inside."

The brothers washed the blood from him and rubbed fat on his wounds.

"Perhaps they will be kind to me now," Hatupatu thought. But when they were ready for their meal, they took birds which had been cooked in fat and ate them, forgetting all about their young brother. After his feast Hatupatu could not have touched another morsel, but he felt unhappy. He went and sat by the fire, and his brothers laughed at him as he sat and coughed and peered at them with his red-rimmed eyes.

The next morning, when he was alone, Hatupatu had another feast, and once again he cut himself until the blood flowed, and lay down on the path.

His brothers looked at him suspiciously, but they carried him inside, and laid him on the bare floor.

The following morning they left the whare as usual, but instead of going into the forest, they hid behind the trees on the edge of the clearing. Presently they saw Hatupatu come out and make a big fire in the earth oven. Then he went into the storehouse and came out with two fat birds which he wrapped in leaves and placed on top of the hot stones.

*Two fat birds which he placed on top of the hot stones*

He put mats and fern fronds on top, and covered the hole with earth.

The sun crept slowly upwards. When it had reached the top of the sky Hatupatu took out the food and ate it. Then he rested, lying on his back in the tall grass. When the first chill wind of the evening sprang up, Hatupatu got to his feet and went into the storehouse. His brothers left their hiding-place and peeped inside. Once again the baskets were overturned and there sat Hatupatu, carefully cutting himself with the sharp point of a spear.

"Ha!" shouted his eldest brother, rushing inside. "See, here is the enemy that robs our storehouse."

He struck him with his club and Hatupatu fell backwards amongst the overturned baskets.

"You have killed him," said the second brother. The other laughed.

"It serves him right for his greediness," he said.

Soon after this, the brothers returned to their home at Rotorua.

"Where is Hatupatu, your little brother?" their father said when he greeted them.

"We do not know," they replied. "He must have gone away last night. We could not find him."

The old man went inside his whare and spoke to his wife.

"Hatupatu is dead. He has been killed by his brothers. I can see it in their eyes, though their tongues say no."

"What shall we do, O my husband?"

"We will find him. I will send a spirit to look for him."

He sang a magic song and presently Tamumu, the blowfly-who-buzzes-in-the-skies, came through the open door.

"Find my son, Hatupatu, whose body is somewhere in the forest," said the old man.

Tamumu flew out and over the hills. Everywhere he could see the tops of the forest trees. After a long time he saw a tiny whare with a little storehouse close by. He flew down and into the storehouse. Inside there was the body of Hatupatu.

He-who-buzzes-in-the-skies crawled under the feathers and sang a song of true magic. After a long while Hatupatu moved one foot and then an arm. He lifted his hands and brushed the feathers from his face. Tamumu flew down, touched his forehead and flew away.

114

Hatupatu stood up and looked round him. He saw that his brothers had gone and that no one was there. He snatched a wooden spear and ran out of the storehouse.

Presently he met an old woman who was killing birds. Instead of thrusting a spear gently through the leaves, as bird hunters do, she speared them with her lips.

Hatupatu knew that she was an ogress. As she crept quietly up to a tree, Hatupatu moved back, but the ogress saw him. A long arm reached towards him, but Hatupatu turned and ran away. At first he thought he had escaped, but when he stopped to listen, he could hear the noise she made as she moved between the trees. He ran faster than ever, but after a while he had to stop and get his breath. Every time he stopped the ogress was nearer than ever, though he could not see her.

Presently he came to the edge of the forest. He ran down a long hill but the ogress was close behind him. He turned his head and saw that she had nearly reached him. There were wings on her arms. She held them out, rising in the air. A moment later her bony fingers clasped his waist and Hatupatu felt himself lifted off the ground. She dragged him along a narrow path, until she came to a broken-down whare, half hidden under a clump of nikau ferns.

"Lie there," she said as she pushed him through the door. Night had fallen quickly and it was dark inside.

In the morning Hatupatu looked round the little room. The ogress was sitting on the floor.

"Stay here," she said. "If you leave this house I will catch you and punish you."

She went out and shut the door behind her. Hatupatu peeped out of the window. He could see the ogress far away on the mountainside, and he knew that if he tried to run away, she would soon catch him. Then he looked round the walls. Beautiful cloaks of birds' feathers and white dogskin were hanging there.

"I would like to have them for myself," he thought. He stretched out his hand, but as he did so there was a flutter of wings, and a bird flew down and pecked his arm. Then he opened the door a little way, and through the crack he saw a lizard watching him with beady eyes. Hatupatu shivered and closed the door quickly, because he was frightened of lizards.

He felt cold and hunted round to see if there was any wood for the fire. Snap! A big brown kiwi stabbed the earth with his long beak, close to Hatupatu's foot.

The boy knew then that the witch had left the birds and the lizards to watch him. He felt angry. Another look through the window showed him that the sun was shining and there was no sign of the ogress.

He snatched a weapon from the walls and hunted through every nook and cranny of the whare until he had found all the witch's birds. Then he opened the door and struck the lizard till it lay still without moving.

Hatupatu took the cloaks down from the walls, and ran quickly into the forest. He ran and ran, until he could run no more. He sat down on the bank of a stream and drank the icy cold water. "She will never find me now," he said to himself.

But there was one bird in the witch's whare he had not seen. It had been hiding under the eaves. As soon as Hatupatu left, this bird flew down over the hills until it found the ogress. It perched on her shoulder and told her that her prisoner had escaped after killing all the other birds, taking the beautiful feather cloaks with him.

The ogress ran swiftly back to the whare. There was no sign of Hatupatu, but the little bird flew on ahead of her, showing the path that Hatupatu had taken.

Hatupatu was feeling rested now. He stood up and looked back along the way he had come. His heart stood still for a moment, for there was the ogress, standing on the hill-top he had left a little while before.

She caught sight of him and gave a shout. The next moment she was rushing down the side of the hill with her arms spread wide apart, floating on the air faster than Hatupatu could run.

He turned and ran as hard as he could. The bush-lawyer clutched him and the manuka scratched him, but he did not feel them. Faster and faster he

*A big brown kiwi stabbed the earth close to Hatupatu's foot*

ran to where the forest trees grew farther apart, and the sun shone in a grassy valley.

"If only I can reach that big rock," Hatupatu gasped as he came out into the sunshine. But a shadow fell across him. It was the shadow of the ogress who was floating in the air above him, waiting to catch him in her long claws.

Hatupatu threw himself against the rock and cried desperately. "Open, rock!" Part of the rock swung back almost like a door, and Hatupatu fell inside. There was a crash as the hole closed up again. It was dark inside the rock and there was hardly room to move, but he felt safe. He could hear the bird woman beating against the stone, trying to claw her way inside. He could even hear the fluttering of the bird's wings. Then came silence. The ogress muttered and growled, but presently the sound died away and all was quiet. A long time went by and everything was still.

"She must have gone," Hatupatu said. He pushed gently against the rock and it opened.* The ogress had gone. Hatupatu knew that he was not far away from home. As the sun was setting he climbed the last hill and saw the lovely sight of

*Part of the rock swung back like a door*

Lake Rotorua below him. The smoke from the ovens, which had been lit for the evening meal, rose straight up in the quiet air. In the middle of the lake was his island home. He ran downhill towards the steaming geysers and mud pools of Whakarewarewa on his way to the lake. Then suddenly he heard the whirr of giant wings. The ogress had caught up with him again!

*Hatupatu's rock can still be seen. It is in the valley where the main road runs from Putaruru to Taupo. You can still see the hole where Hatupatu hid. Travellers still put a sprig of teatree in the hole as a good luck charm on their journey just as the Maori did before them for hundreds of years.

Hatupatu ran along the narrow path between the boiling mud pools. The bird woman had stretched out her talons to seize Hatupatu when a cloud of steam blinded her. Hatupatu felt her as she brushed past him – and a moment later she fell into the boiling mud pool and sank from sight.

* * *

There was a gasp, and a sigh of relief from the children.

"More," they shouted. "Tell us more about Hatupatu."

"No," said Popo firmly. "That was a good story, but another would spoil it. It would be like eating more kumaras when you have had enough.

"If you are good children and help gather firewood, perhaps Rangi will tell you another story tonight. What do you say to that, Rangi?" The good-natured story-teller from Rotorua laughed softly and his eyes twinkled. "If there is a big pile of wood by sundown," he said, "yes, then I will tell you another story."

# TUTANEKAI WHO PLAYED THE FLUTE

POPO had taken Rangi across to the island in the harbour, and with them had gone Hine and Rata and more than twenty other girls and boys. It had been fun exploring the island while the two men gathered the oysters which clustered thickly on the rocks.

When the sun was high in the sky, it was so hot that everyone was glad to sit in the shade of the big pohutukawa at the end of the little beach on the north side of the island.

"Can we have another story about Hatupatu?" Rata asked, as he lay along the branch of the pohutukawa which hung over the bay and dabbled his fingers in the water.

"No, I don't think so," Rangi said lazily. "There are plenty of other adventures that Hatupatu had, but it is too hot."

"Oh, please tell us about your home," Hine pleaded. "It's on an island too, like this one, isn't it?"

"It's bigger," Rangi said. "Much bigger, just as the lake is bigger than your harbour."

"What is its name?" one of the older boys asked.

"Mokoia."

"That's where Hatupatu lived, isn't it?" Rata asked quickly.

"Yes, and many other great people."

"What were their names?"

"Oh, there was Tutanekai, who played the flute."

"That sounds as though it could be a good story," Popo said. "Go on, Rangi. I've told the children so many stories that my tongue is nearly worn out. I would like to hear it too."

"Oh well," said Rangi, settling himself more comfortably on the sand, "if I leave the story of Tutanekai and his flute with you, it will be my gift to the boys and girls. This is the story."

\* \* \*

Tutanekai was a young chief and, as I have told you, he lived on the island of Mokoia. Round the edge of Lake Rotorua are many little villages, and the canoes of Mokoia sometimes visited them and brought back news of what was happening. On the marae tales were told of the lovely young women who lived in these villages. There was one name that was spoken more often than any other. It was Hinemoa, the beautiful young woman who lived at Owhata.

Tutanekai and his brothers loved to hear about her, although they had never seen her. Because they had heard so much about her beauty and gentleness, they fell in love with her. Each brother boasted that he would marry her some day, but Tutanekai said nothing. At night he went out on to the balcony of his hillside whare and looked across the dark water towards Owhata. Then he would sigh and for a little while he played on his flute.

The tender love notes carried clearly across the water in the still air. Sometimes Hinemoa heard them as she sat with her friends in the moonlight. She had heard of the brothers of Mokoia, and when the music crept across to Owhata she would smile and say, "That is Tutanekai's flute."

One day the people of Mokoia paid a visit to Owhata, and Tutanekai was amongst them. As soon as he saw the high-born Hinemoa, he knew who she was, and in the same way she recognised the tall, handsome young chief as the flute-player of Mokoia.

That night they met in the shadow of the meeting-house.

"How shall we meet again?" Tutanekai asked the young woman.

"I will come to you, Tutanekai," Hinemoa said softly. "My people will not allow me to marry you, but some night I will come to you. How shall I know when you will be waiting?"

Tutanekai thought for a moment. "Already my music has carried the message of my love to you across the waters of the lake. Now it can carry another message – the message that I am waiting for you. When you hear the music you will know that I am waiting."

The next day the visitors from Mokoia returned home. That night, when it was dark and all the people were asleep, Hinemoa crept down to the beach and looked for a small canoe which she could paddle across to the island. But the canoes had all been pulled out of the water and were well up the beach. Even the smallest of them was too heavy for her to drag down by herself. Then she knew that the old people had seen how she had looked at Tutanekai, and had done this to stop her from going to him.

As she stood by the lake edge the music of the flute came clearly across the water. Hinemoa turned sadly and went back to her whare. Night after night she went down to the beach as the notes of the flute came from Mokoia, but the canoes were always far up on the beach.

Tutanekai was still waiting, but perhaps he would soon think that she had forgotten him!

*They met in the shadow of the meeting-house*

At last she could wait no longer. If there were no canoes, she would swim! But it was a long way to Mokoia, and the night was dark. In order that she could swim she took off her cloak, tied some empty gourds under her arms and waded out into the water.

She could not see anything, but the music of Tutanekai's flute came out of the darkness to guide her. She swam on steadily but little waves splashed against her face, and presently she could hear the music no longer. The water was cold and she felt frightened, not knowing where she was.

There was only one thing to do – to keep on swimming. Once more she heard Tutanekai's music. The water grew colder, the music stopped, and now there was only the sound

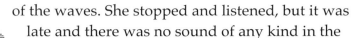

of the waves. She stopped and listened, but it was late and there was no sound of any kind in the night. Suddenly she heard a new sound. It was the sound of waves lapping on at stony beach. She swam on quickly, and soon she reached the beach. The wind was colder than the water, but she went on, feeling her way with her hands in front of her. She brushed through low bushes, and felt the rocks. They were warm and she could smell the steam from a hot pool.

Then she knew where she was. The hot pool was not far from Tutanekai's whare. She stepped into it and lay down so that the water warmed her cold body. She thought of Tutanekai and felt shy. Her clothes were far away on the beach at Owhata, and she did not dare to go up to her lover's house.

Then she heard someone coming. In a flash she hid behind a rock. She could not see anything but she heard footsteps and a splash as a calabash was lowered into the pool. Talking in a deep voice like a man, she said,

"Where are you taking the water? Who are you?"

The man who was getting water was startled. "I am taking the water to Tutanekai," he said.

"Give me the calabash," Hinemoa said, still in a deep voice.

She waded up to him and took the calabash. Then she threw it away so that it crashed on to the rocks and broke.

The slave cried out angrily, "Why have you done that? That was Tutanekai's calabash!"

Hinemoa did not answer, but hid behind the rocks again. The slave thought that she might have been a warrior, or perhaps an evil spirit.

He ran quickly back to the house and told Tutanekai what had happened.

"Who broke the calabash?" Tutanekai asked.

"The man in the pool."

"Yes, but who was he?"

"I don't know. It was a man, but I couldn't see his face."

For a moment Tutanekai thought of going down to see for himself but

*She waded up to him and took the calabash*

changed his mind. What did it matter? For night after night he had played to Hinemoa, and night after night he had strained his eyes trying to see her canoe. But she had not come to him. Perhaps she had forgotten him!

"It doesn't matter," he said to the slave. "Take another calabash, but see that you bring it back this time."

The slave went down to the pool again, but as soon as he reached the water the deep voice said, "If that is Tutanekai's calabash, give it to me!"

"No, I must take it back again."

"Give it to me," Hinemoa said, fiercely, and the slave, who still feared that she might be a fairy or a goblin, handed it over. Hinemoa broke it on a rock. This time the slave did not wait. He ran up the path and stumbled into the whare.

"The second calabash has gone," he said to his master. "It was the man in the hot pool who did it."

"Never mind," Tutanekai said wearily. "We have plenty of calabashes. Take another and see how you get on this time."

The slave was soon back empty-handed once more. This time Tutanekai was really angry. "I will soon put a stop to this," he said. He threw off his sleeping-mat, took his mere (club) and ran down to the pool.

Hinemoa heard him coming, and knew that it was her lover. The slave's footsteps had been heavy and slow, while Tutanekai ran lightly and swiftly.

*The second calabash had gone!*

She hid still farther behind the rocks, and held her breath as the young man reached the edge of the pool. The moon was rising and she saw his shadow lying across the water, but she was hidden behind the rocks.

"Where are you, breaker of pots?" called Tutanekai. "Come out so that I can see you. Show yourself like a man, instead of hiding like a crayfish in the water."

Hinemoa did not answer. She watched the shadow moving across the water, coming closer and closer. A hand reached down and touched her hair.

"Ah ha!" said Tutanekai thinking that he

had found the rascal who had broken his calabashes. "Come out into the light and fight like a man !"

He pulled harder and said angrily, "Let me see your face."

Then Hinemoa stood up shyly, like the white heron which is seen only once in a hundred years. She climbed out of the pool and stood in the bright moonlight.

The mere fell from Tutanekai's hand and dangled by the flax string. He stepped back in amazement, and then held out his arms. A moment later Hinemoa was at last safe in the arms of her lover. Hand in hand they went up the path to Tutanekai's home and became man and wife together. No one else knew that Hinemoa had come to Mokoia; no one but Hinemoa and Tutanekai knew that the lovers had met and had been married that night.

The next morning the sun rose and soon the steam from the ovens rose straight up in the still air, as the people ate their morning meal. Suddenly someone noticed that Tutanekai was not there.

"Where is he?" they asked, but no one had seen him.

"There is his slave," an old woman said. "Let us ask him."

They called the slave over to them and asked him where his master was.

"I do not know," he said. "The door of his whare is closed, and I have not seen him since he went down to see the stranger at the pool last night."

"What stranger?" he was asked.

The slave told them how he had gone down to the pool and how the calabashes had been broken by some stranger whom he had not seen in the darkness.

"Tutanekai was angry," the slave said. "He told me to stay here, and then he took his mere and went down to see the stranger himself."

The people looked at each other. An old man got up and walked up and down in front of the others. At last he stopped and looked at them.

"These are strange words," he said. "Perhaps something has happened to Tutanekai. He is a brave fighter, but it was a dark night. The stranger may well have been an enemy who lay in wait for Tutanekai. Perhaps he has been killed. I say that one of the young men should go down to the pool to see if he is there."

A younger man stood up. "The words of my father are wise," he said. "In the dark night even the bravest man may be beaten by the thrust of a hidden spear. But perhaps it did not happen like that at all. Perhaps Tutanekai is still in his whare. See, the door is still shut, as his slave has said. I say that we should look first in his whare."

"Ae!" said the people. "Let us look there first."

The slave went over to the whare. He slid the door back and looked inside for a long time.

"He cannot see inside until his eyes get used to the darkness," said the young chief who had spoken last.

Presently the slave turned and came to the edge of the veranda. He spoke softly but everyone could hear him, because they were so quiet.

"There are four feet there," he said. "I looked for Tutanekai and I saw four feet instead of two."

"Who is with him?" an old woman called.

The slave turned back and looked through the door again. He went right inside, and then came out again and walked down to where the people were sitting. They could see that he was excited.

"I have seen her! It is Hinemoa!"

"Hinemoa who lives at Owhata?" the old woman asked.

"Yes. It is the young woman whom Tutanekai has been courting. She has heard the sound of his flute and has come to him across the lake."

The people were excited too. "It is Hinemoa," they shouted. "Welcome to Hinemoa."

That night Hinemoa told them how she had crossed the lake, swimming through the dark water, guided by the music of Tutanekai's flute.

* * *

"And that story," said Rangi, "has been told over and over again through the years. As long as the little island of Mokoia rests on Lake Rotorua, the Arawa people will remember the story of Hinemoa and Tutanekai."

"Ah, we should like to see your island," Popo said, "and the hot pool where Hinemoa hid because she was so shy."

"I should like you to see the geysers, too. They are very much like your blowhole. You can hear a rumbling far under the earth and then there is a great eruption of water and steam – but it is boiling water, and we have to be careful not to stand too close to it."

"It would be fun to have boiling water everywhere," Hine said. "You could cook food and wash clothes in it."

Rangi smiled. "Yes, our women use the boiling pools to cook their food and to wash their clothes. And we can wash ourselves in them, too. Some of the pools are warm and not too hot. On cold winter nights we stay in the pools for hours to keep ourselves warm. Some day you may visit us, and then we will show you wonderful things in our part of the country, where the fire gods lie close beneath the ground, and we tame them to make them help us to cook our food."

"Well," said Popo. "We are glad to have heard these stories of Rotorua. You may all run away and play, while Rangi and I talk of olden days and the strange things we have seen together. Some day perhaps we will all go there, when the kumaras have been harvested and the tribes are at peace."

# ENDNOTE

The stories and illustrations in this book were previously published by
A. H. & A. W. Reed in two volumes, *Wonder Tales of Maoriland (Aotearoa /
New Zealand)* and *Maori Tales of Long Ago,* both illustrated by A. S. Paterson,
whose other work was published regularly by *The Dominion* newspaper in
Wellington.

The skill of the story-teller, A. W. Reed, is evident in the fact that his original
versions are equally relevant and readable in this 21st century edition,
published by New Holland. Very nearly all of the original illustrations are
published throughout this edition. David Simmons' Foreword is new.

A longer collection of 28 chapters, with 50 full-page illustrations by Dennis
Turner and cover design by Cliff Whiting, is *Myths and Legends of Maoriland,*
now titled *Maori Myths and Legendary Tales,* which is also published by New
Holland and is the most popular collection of Maori ancestral tales, with over
50,000 copies in print.

Ray Richards (1921-2013)
*Former vice-chairman, A. H. & A. W. Reed Ltd.*
*Booksellers New Zealand/Publishers Association of New Zealand Lifetime Achievement Award 2011.*